AMBUSH
AT
DEVIL'S WHIP

AMBUSH
AT
DEVIL'S WHIP

•

James Rhodes

AVALON BOOKS
NEW YORK

PRINTED IN THE UNITED STATES OF AMERICA
ON ACID-FREE PAPER
BY HADDON CRAFTSMEN, BLOOMSBURG, PENNSYLVANIA

To Georgia Ray, William G. Seif and Avis Mueller

Chapter One

Gordy Witcher's leg was bothering him today. He stretched it out as far as he could in what little space he had on the driver's side of the stagecoach. He wished he was in Clovis with Rose Gonzales and they were drinking cheap wine and beer and she was cuddled close to him with that wild fragrance she wore which made his head go crazy. Instead he had to pay attention to his driving. It was a long haul from Denver to Valiant and the road was getting rougher and rougher. Ahead of them stretched the handle of Devil's Whip that warned him of the twisting, winding road which lay ahead. "Red" Robbins was riding shotgun and Red never said any extra words. Not to Gordy, not to anyone.

1

Reaching down, Gordy scratched the area of his leg that was bothering him. It had been an old wound he had received in Chickamauga in the War serving under Rosecrans when some fragments of an exploding cannonball nearly severed his leg below the kneecap. It had healed but whenever the weather turned the least bit chilly, as it had now that the stagecoach was beginning to climb to a higher elevation, the ragged, white scar kicked up and gave him pain and a pronounced limp.

Gordy gee-upped the team of four horses and slapped the reins so they made a snapping sound that echoed through the Wyoming air. Gordy spit a wad of tobacco juice over the side and it fell with a brownish glint into the chasm creeping up on the right side of the coach.

Inside the anything but plush interior the lone woman passenger was doing her best to read from the book her husband had given her before she had left Valiant for Denver. She had spent a month at her sister's house where she had made herself useful after the mistress of the house had given birth to her firstborn: a strapping, florid-faced bundle of flesh who was a thief. An outrageous thief who had stolen not only the hearts of his father and mother but of his visiting aunt who, herself, longed for the day when she too would bring life into the world.

The woman smiled as she thought about her sister and the baby and of her own husband who would not miss her during the daylight hours since he was a diligent and hard-working rancher. It was only at night when she knew that he missed the warmth of her body as much as she missed his. The hours, after supper, when she would read to him from whatever books she had managed to bring with her when she had left the comfort and security of her home in Virginia to come to this windswept, uncompromising land with its sky-climbing mountains and its cold, relentless winter blizzards.

"You've kept your nose in that book ever since we left Denver," the man sitting opposite her finally said. "Must be a very interesting story."

This abruptly brought the woman out of the world of Bulwer-Lytton's *Last Days of Pompeii*.

"What did you say?" she asked and smiled at the older man who dressed conservatively but well. Obviously a man with breeding. "I sometimes get lost in a book that I enjoy."

"I've noticed that. Are you going to Valiant too?"

"My husband will be meeting the coach. I've been visiting my sister and her husband in Denver."

The man listened attentively. He had the ability to bring people out of themselves. He was an excellent and obedient listener. "Did you have an advantageous visit?"

"It couldn't have been better. I became an aunt for the first time."

This brought an ever wider smile to the older man's lips. He must have had children and could possibly be a grandparent. The woman felt safe with the man; he exuded warmth and understanding.

The woman glanced at the two other passengers: a bearded, grizzled miner who had fallen asleep from the moment he had entered the coach, and a young man with a bandaged head who had come out second best in a barroom brawl. The young man just sat with his hand to his jaw and softly moaned every time the coach bounced over a ragged section of the road.

"You say your husband is going to meet you at Valiant?" the older man said. "Does he live there?"

"We have a small spread of land outside of town," the woman volunteered.

"Wyoming is starting to grow," the older man said. "I hear that Valiant has its own bank. That usually is a good indication a city is starting to prosper. Yes, Wyoming is beginning to stretch out."

The woman closed the book and rested her hands on it in her lap. She was very pretty with periwinkle blue eyes, her best feature, which snapped with warm wit and intelligence. Whoever the man was that was married to her, the older man thought, he must be very lucky. She began to speak in a soft, feminine voice about how she had met her husband and how they had courted. Every time she made reference to him it was with such a loving manner, it was obvious she was still in love.

"We must be nearing the mountain pass," the older man said. He had noticed how the coach had begun to sway and jostle as the horses strained against their harnesses.

The woman glanced out the window of the coach. "Devil's Whip. I always get a little nervous on this part of the trip. You don't dare cross over Devil's Whip after the snow falls. It's just too dangerous."

She needn't have said this because the older man had clutched the portmanteau closer to his vest as though it were some sort of talisman that would ward off any danger which might threaten him.

Gordy Witcher wasn't paying any attention to the pain in his leg now. He had forgotten the aching just as soon as the first serpentine curve of Devil's Whip came upon the stagecoach. He wished now that he hadn't stayed up so late last night. He wished he was in Valiant and that this ordeal was behind him.

Ahead of the stagecoach a man hiding behind an outcropping of sandstone rock checked the kerchief he had wound around his face so that only his eyes could be seen beneath the brim of his Stetson. He was nervous. But it was a cautious kind of nervousness. He had been in this situation or similar situations before. It was his job and he was good at his job. He could hear the sound of the horses as they lumbered along the narrow rock-strewn road. He closed his eyes for a moment and he could almost visualize the pile of gold he was going to receive for this day's work. And that was what he considered what he was doing, just work. When he opened his eyes he reached for the Winchester .44-40 and made certain there were bullets in the chamber.

He had planned ahead what would happen. The horses would be spooked and that would throw off the driver. He would have to put a bullet in him and the man riding shotgun. That didn't bother the shooter; he had killed other men before. He looked over his shoulder to make certain the man who had hired him was still in the shadows. He nodded to let the man know it was just a matter of minutes.

Gordy Witcher and Red Robbins didn't feel a thing when the bullets entered their skulls and made clean, quick exits through the backs of their heads. The horses reared in fright and panic, their heated breaths making white vaporous etchings against the early morning chill.

Inside the coach the passengers had just a moment of terror before the coach crashed over the side of the mountain, killing them almost instantly as it struck a jagged-edged mound of sandstone. It was over in seconds and the dying team of horses whinnied their last as the wheels of the coach spun round and round, slowly coming to one last, final revolution.

Chapter Two

It wasn't until two days after his wife's death that Tom Cardy heard about it. A lone rider had been on the twisting Devil's Whip and he had come across the wreckage of the stagecoach. He had climbed down the side of the steep cliff but there was nothing he could do for any of the passengers or the horses. One of the male passenger's face was so badly mangled that it made him sick to look at it. He had spurred his red roan gelding into a fast and dangerous gallop until he had reached Valiant. There he had gone quickly to the marshal and told him what he had discovered on Devil's Whip.

Gathering a small posse of men and some three wagons, they had climbed the road and fended their way through the minor avalanches until they had come to the wreckage.

"It's Tom Cardy's Caroline," one of the men had said. "He had said something about her being on the stage from Denver."

"He'll take this real hard," Marshal Ben Yoder had said and shook his head in disbelief. Ben was a close friend of Tom Cardy. They had been born and reared in Wyoming, had ridden out the lonely duty of line camps together many times before Tom settled down to married life and Ben was elected marshal.

Ben knew Caroline too. She was a sweet, gentle woman who had loved Tom Cardy and was making a good home for him on that spread of land just north of Valiant. Tom wouldn't take this too well. Ben hated to be the one to break the news to Tom, but he wouldn't allow anyone else to do it.

The bodies were wrapped in oilcloth and placed in the wagons that now were used as makeshift hearses. Ben thought it was an unceremonious end to what might have been prosperous lives.

Ben had known Gordy Witcher and for him, at least, it wasn't a surprising finish to a rather disreputable existence. Nonetheless it was a very solemn procession from Devil's Whip, down the incline and across the wide expanse of grassy land to Valiant.

"Ain't no accident, Marshal," one of the grizzled men had said when he had turned Gordy Witcher and Red Robbins over and seen the gunshot wounds to their heads. "Good, clean shootin'."

Ben had found the spent cartridges from the Winchester near the place where the bushwhacker had lain in wait. He stored them in his vest pocket for whatever good they might do in the future. At least here was proof that it hadn't been some accidental shooting from some misguided hunter.

Tom Cardy would have joined the men but, as Ben knew, he had suffered an accident only the day before and was in bed, his leg swollen and too painful for him to either walk or ride. Tom had been in his office when he learned the stagecoach from Denver was not on time. This wasn't unusual, but Tom Cardy wasn't the type of man who could wait with patience.

"There must be something wrong, Ben," Tom had said to him that day. "The stagecoach should have been here hours ago."

"Settle down, Tom," Ben had said. "You tell me when the stagecoach is ever on time. Don't worry, Caroline will make it here all right."

"I'll hold you to that," Tom had replied, his face set in hard, serious lines. Then, like he had done ever since Ben had known him, he broke into a wide, ingratiating grin. "Until you cry for mercy."

"Have a cup of coffee, you deranged drover," Ben had joked.

"If I have any more coffee I won't sleep for a year."

"Good. Then maybe you'll get some work done on that ranch of yours."

Tom smirked. "I can outdo you, Ben Yoder, any day of the week when it comes to hard labor. Don't you forget that."

That was how it always went when the two of them got together. They were as close as brothers and sometimes just as ornery. When they were still in school their pranks were the talk of Valiant. What one of them didn't think of doing, the other would. They were the bane of many a teacher and nobody would have given any odds that the two of them would grow up to be such stalwart citizens.

What had brought about the change in Tom Cardy was his meeting with Caroline Thurman. In a matter of days his entire life had taken a complete turnaround. What he thought before about life and a devil-may-care attitude, had vanished. All he could think about, all his mind could dwell upon, was how he could get Caroline to see him as responsible and a bastion of common sense and uprightness. He wrote her letters in that awkward, almost indecipherable scrawl and hand-delivered them. It became a private source of amusement between them. Caroline had pointed out some grammatical errors and Tom had taken to signing his letters with a crude, squiggly X that became his own official signature.

Ben had become best man at their wedding and had proudly worn his tin star that glittered and winked in the light from the candles.

Tom and Caroline began their married life in a one-room lean-to that Tom had built with the help of Ben and some of the men from Valiant. Their bed was a mattress of feedsacks stuffed with Montana feathers. But within a few months Tom had built a ranch house and furnished it with comfortable chairs and tables. There was even glass in the windows. For the first year of their marriage Ben was a regular visitor for some of Caroline's mouth-watering suppers and he was just as entranced as her husband when, after eating, she got out one of the books she had brought from Virginia and read a chapter to them. It was more the sound of Caroline's soft, tender voice that kept Tom interested than the contents of what she read.

Ben was the one who would remark some days later when he saw Tom, "That was a great chapter

Caroline read us the other night on Natty Bumppo, wasn't it, Tom."

Tom assured Ben that it was. Ben knew that Tom really hadn't heard a word that Caroline had spoken from the great James Fenimore Cooper and he liked to josh Tom.

"That Sir Walter Scott is really some writer," Ben would say. "None better, don't you think."

Tom would wait for a few seconds and then reply, "You're right, Ben, almost as good as James Fenimore Cooper. We ought to get Caroline to read some of his stuff one of these nights."

That was when Ben would toss whatever was handy at Tom.

Ben rode back to Valiant with a heavy heart. He would find the murderer of Caroline Cardy, Gordy Witcher, Red Robbins, and the three unknowns that he and the men had found in the wreckage. Ben had a fairly good idea who the miner might be, although he couldn't be certain. But the fancy-dressed Eastern dude with the mangled face and the boy with the bandaged head he was completely in the dark on.

The wagons moved morosely and cautiously along the tip of Devil's Whip. From experience the drivers knew that this was still treacherous going. Almost as though the weather was in mourning too, the sky was filled with dark, gray-swelled clouds. Ben wondered if they might get rained or snowed on before they reached Valiant. At this time of the year it wasn't easy to gauge what the weather might be in Wyoming.

It was a solemn procession that inched its way down the side of the mountain. All of the men in the party knew Tom and his wife. Some of the men were married and they knew what it would mean to lose someone they loved and cherished. Not many words were spoken and Ben was glad of this. It gave him time to think, to try to come to some reasonable explanation of why this had happened. The bushwacker who had ambushed the stagecoach was probably long gone by this time.

"Marshal." One of the men interrupted his thoughts. "Where we gonna put these here bodies?"

For a moment Ben found it hard to think of Caroline Cardy as just a body. Then he said, "Undertaker. Josh Merkin'll know what to do with them."

"Some of us married think we ought to ask our wives to bring over some food for Tom. What do you think?"

"Tom would appreciate it," Ben said. "Whether he knows it now or not."

That burst of talk seemed to break the somber mood of the party. The men then began to talk more openly among themselves. Ben heard them saying what they would do if they ever caught up with whoever did this to Gordy, Red, and Caroline. Ben heard words from, "string 'em up" and "hanging's too good for whoever did this" to, "just give me five minutes alone with him. Me and my jackknife. Won't need no necktie party then."

Ben listened and agreed in his heart but he had to say, "There'll be no stringin' up and no cuttin' with any knives. The law will handle this. Even if we don't like that too much. Can't have us takin' things into our own hands. Much as we'd like to."

Ben wasn't sure his voice was all that convincing. Still, he had to uphold the law, even if he disagreed with it in his gut.

After that Ben occasionally caught the looks that some of them aimed at him. He knew that none of them would go against the law; maybe Ben Yoker, but never the law. Ben wasn't too worried since he stood over six-five and was as muscular as a summer-fed bear. Besides that, there wasn't a man in Valiant who could outdraw him except maybe Tom Cardy. Ben knew he could intimidate and he didn't give a damn.

"How do you think Tom will take this?" one of the men said not necessarily to Ben.

Ben didn't turn in the direction of the voice.

"How would you take it?" was all he said and it didn't require an answer.

By the time they had reached the end of Devil's Whip most of the men had gotten over their antagonism toward Ben. Ben knew all of them, some were classmates, and they knew the burly marshal never carried a grudge and could put just about any insult or slur behind him.

"If you want, Ben," a man said, "we'll take the bodies to Josh Merkin's. No need you having to go to all that trouble. Particularly since you have to go tell Tom about his missus."

"Thanks," Ben said and smiled at the man, who nodded his head in tacit agreement.

"We'll have to keep the bodies of the other three passengers on ice until we can get some identification. Don't have any idea who to notify that they're dead," Ben added.

Tom Cardy was in bed worrying. He was worrying about the cattle which weren't being tended right, or leastwise the way he would tend them. He was worrying about the house not looking the way his wife would want it to. But mostly he was worrying about Caroline. The stagecoach was now two days overdue. He was afraid something really bad had befallen the coach and its passengers.

"Brought you some soup," Abbie Dusault,

Tom's nearest neighbor's wife said. Abbie had taken it upon herself to bring Tom some food since the accident that had laid him up. Abbie was a better cook than she was a housekeeper but Tom Cardy appreciated all that she was doing for him. "Here's a bowl and some sourdough bread. I'll leave it right here for you. Better keep up your strength, Tom."

"Thanks, Abbie. I don't know what I would have done if it hadn't been for you and Andy since I got laid up."

Abbie waved him off with a quick flick of her hand.

"We're neighbors. You and Caroline have been real good to Andy and me and the boys. I'm going to see about cleaning up the place before Caroline gets back from Denver."

At the mention of his wife's name that feeling of dread came back to Tom. Why did he feel this way? He hadn't had one bit of worry when she had boarded the stage for Denver. Tom drifted back to that day when he had taken Caroline to catch the stagecoach. He had had a surprise for her.

"What's this?" Caroline had asked when he handed her the brown-wrapped package.

"Open it and see."

Caroline had slowly opened the package and

she almost dropped the book when she saw what Tom had given her.

"Oh, Tom, thank you," Caroline had said and she gave him a quick kiss as she pressed hard on his hand.

It was a first edition of *The Last Days of Pompeii*, which Tom had been saving for a Christmas gift. But this was a special occasion and Christmas would be just another reason for him to give Caroline something else.

"Even autographed it for you," Tom had said and a sly smile cracked his lips. "But you'll have to hunt for it."

"There'll be plenty of time for that on the trip to Denver," Caroline said. "You going to be all right?"

Tom made a face, wrinkling his forehead by squeezing his eyebrows together. Then he grinned.

"If you think I'm going to miss you," Tom said, jutting his chin forward, "you're right. How long you aimin' on stayin' at your sister's?"

"For as long as I'm needed. You don't mind me going, do you, Tom?"

Tom assured his wife he didn't mind, even though if the truth could be uttered, he did. But that was only for selfish reasons. Anyway, Caroline wouldn't be gone forever. After the baby came she would be catching the next stagecoach for Valiant. He could survive until she came back.

It was Abbie who saw Ben Yoder ride up and tether his horse to the hitching rail outside the house.

"Marshal Yoder's here, Tom," Abbie said before she went to answer the door.

Tom wondered what Ben was doing here again. He had been coming every day since the accident and Tom knew he had other business to attend to. Not that he minded company, it got kind of testy-like lying here with nothing to do.

He heard the front door open and then some mumbling before Ben walked into the room. Tom knew from the moment Ben stood there framed by the light that came in from the window that something had happened. In the other room, Abbie heard a choking, muffled sound that she mistook for Tom laughing at some joke Ben was making.

Tom was on crutches when the burial services were held for Caroline. He didn't remember much of the service since he had been in a foggy daze ever since Ben had told him about Caroline's death.

"Sorry about your wife's death, Tom," Jubal Johnson, manager of the local bank, said. "If there's anything I can do, just let me know."

"Thanks, Mr. Johnson," Tom had said. Jubal, as usual, avoided looking directly at Tom. Tom couldn't remember when he had ever had direct eye contact with the banker.

"I'm going back to the ranch with you," said Jack Madrid. Jack was in his late forties, bearded, single, and for once not smelling like a week-dead polecat.

Tom didn't protest; he couldn't. He was still numb and just moving through his grief and loss. Ben Yoder rode alongside them in solemn quietude. Tom was about as tall as Ben. He was fair while Ben was dark, and Tom's hair touched his shoulders which Ben's once had. That was before Tom married and Ben became marshal. Like other cowhands their long hair was for good reasons. It kept their ears warm when they slept on the cold Wyoming ground. Many a cowhand had gone deaf from going unprotected and letting the cold ground do its deadly business.

A moaning wind whispered through the trailside brush and sent spirals of grainy dust into the air. Out across the open fields the mountains stood in ancient grandeur with patches of early winter snow sparkling from the brilliant rays of the sun.

When they got to the ranch Tom invited the two men inside. Abbie, with the help of some of the townswomen, spread the living-room table with plates of chicken, potato salads, spicy beans, and warm, homemade bread.

"Help yourselves," Tom said.

"Only if you join us," Ben replied. He watched Tom to make certain he ate and kept his strength up.

"I'm not hungry . . . but I'll try some of this stuff. For Abbie's sake," Tom said and Ben made sure that Tom piled his plate high with food.

As they ate Tom began to talk. He slowly got over the mourning he had been going through and in its place was a burning desire to find out what had happened on Devil's Whip, and who was behind Caroline's death.

"You got any leads?" Tom asked then took a bite of chicken.

Ben shook his head. "So far, nothing. I've been busy trying to put names to those other passengers."

"I'm going to find out who did this," Tom said. "Somebody will pay for what they did to Caroline."

Jack Madrid sat next to Tom. When Tom had said these words he glanced first at Tom and then Ben. Jack could see that Ben didn't like what Tom had said. He was afraid that Tom might go off and do something on his own.

"They will," said Ben. "Only I'm the one

who'll find out who did this. I know what you're going through, Tom. Believe me."

Tom took a sip of coffee.

"Do you?"

Ben released a big sigh. Like he'd been holding something inside for a long, long time. "Promise me you won't take the law in your own hands? Will you do that for me, Tom?"

Jack took a big bite from the bread and the crumbs stuck to his mouth as he chewed and kept glancing from Tom to Ben.

"I can't promise anything right now, Ben. Don't you know that?"

"Suppose so. Just think about what I said, will you, huh?"

"I'll think about it."

"Fair enough."

Ben released another big sigh, like some great weight had been lifted from his wide shoulders. "Think I'll have some more of those beans. That Abigail is a real mean cook."

"Save some for me," Jack said as he followed Ben to the table.

Tom was busy eating and Ben uttered something to Jack under his breath. "Why don't you hang around for a while? Sort of watch out for Tom. He's still not too steady on his legs."

"What do you charge to read palms?" Jack said. "I was planning on doing just that. I might even bunk here for a few days. Beats that fleabag I'm living in in town."

They thought they had been fairly quiet when they had exchanged words but Tom looked over at them and said, "I was just going to ask Jack to stick around. Not as a nursemaid but for somebody to jaw with."

That done, Jack and Ben settled down to eat their chow. Nothing more was said about Caroline's death or what had happened on Devil's Whip. Ben left with the feeling that Tom might have just been talking out of his hat, that he really had no plans on tracking down the bushwacker.

"If you need anything, anything at all, just let me know," Ben said as he eased his massive frame into the saddle. "I can still herd cows like a good drover."

"You were never any good at that and you know it," Tom teased.

"Just because I had you for a teacher," were Ben's parting words as he reined his horse and headed back to Valiant.

Tom and Jack stood on the wooden porch and watched Ben Yoder ride away. They stood there not saying a word to each other until Ben had become just a slowly fading figure on the horizon.

Without speaking again they turned and went back inside the house.

"You can take the bedroom," Tom said. "I'll bunk out here."

Jack shook his head. "I'm staying and I'm sleeping right here on the floor. All I need is a blanket. Otherwise no deal."

Tom knew better than to argue with Jack Madrid. The grizzled, hard-as-mountain-rock drover wouldn't back down once he set his mind to something.

Later that night, before they blew out the lamps, Jack said, "When we gonna get the feller that done in Caroline?"

Tom steadied himself with a crutch and then said, "Just as soon as this leg heals. We start hunting."

Chapter Three

Because Tom Cardy was anxious to find his wife's murderer, the healing of his leg seemed to accelerate. Within a week he and Jack had found temporary help to watch over the cattle and the ranchhouse. They saddled up their horses and rode into town.

"We'll steer clear of the marshal's office," Tom said. "Ben is nobody's fool. He'll know what we're up to."

"You're right there, Tom," Jack said. "Sometimes I think Ben Yoker must have eyes in the back of his head and has some kind of sixth sense about things."

Tom didn't answer Jack because he knew what the man was talking about. Right now, though, he didn't need anybody trying to talk him out of what he had in mind.

Valiant was about an hour's ride from Tom's spread. As he and Jack Madrid rode along he looked at the mountains standing against the horizon. It was late autumn and there was already a dusting of snow on the higher peaks. A wandering wind whined through the tips of the prairie grass and it made a lonesome, melancholy refrain.

The initial shock of Caroline's death was buried in the past. In his way Tom Cardy was still mourning his wife's death. But he knew he wouldn't end that mourning until he found the man who was responsible for her killing. It just made sense to Tom. This would be the completion of the circle.

"What are we doing here?" Jack asked when they rode into Valiant.

"Just look around and ask questions. Listen a lot," Tom said. "No telling what we might pick up."

"No trouble in that," Jack said. "No trouble at all."

"I got to go to the bank for some business." Tom moved his leg in the stirrup. It was still sore even though the leg was mostly healed.

"I'll mosey about town and see what I can pick up."

Tom eased himself out of the saddle and favored his bad leg, getting it out of the stirrup.

A woman and her husband were passing by and they paused for a moment to tell Tom how sorry they were about Caroline. Tom touched the brim of his Stetson in acknowledgement and thanks, then they moved on down the planks that had been set up to keep the townspeople from being swallowed up by dust.

Inside the Valiant City Bank and Trust Tom went directly to the cashier. She was an elderly woman who once was the postmistress but had given up that job when the bank came into town.

"Morning, Tom," the cashier said. "Really was sorry about what happened to Caroline. Guess you know that everyone here is just as upset about this as you are."

Tom doubted this but he managed a thank-you and a smile. Glancing around while the transaction was taking place, Tom caught the eye of Jubal Johnson who was in the manager's office and seemed to be all alone. The smile on Jubal's face was fragmentary and just a little false. But Tom was used to that. Jubal Johnson was not the sort of person who made friends easily, nor was he the socializing kind.

Jubal Johnson had come to the bank as a cashier and in no time had worked himself up to bank manager. There was no doubt in anyone's mind in Valiant that he was shrewd and crafty. But, and Tom had to give this to Jubal, he was hard-working and tenacious.

Tom was about to leave when Jubal waved to him to wait up.

"Can I offer you a cup of coffee, Tom?" Jubal said.

Tom was tempted to accept the coffee since he had had only one cup that morning. However, he did not know what Jack was up to and so he declined.

"But I'll take a raincheck if that's all right," Tom said. He was just leaving the door open in case he had to talk to Jubal Johnson about Caroline and anything he might know about what happened at Devil's Whip.

"Sure. Anytime, Tom," Jubal said. "Drop over to my place anytime you feel like it. I can give you something a little stronger than coffee, if you've a mind to drink it."

This was such an unexpected thing to come from the mouth of Jubal Johnson that Tom was almost flabbergasted. In all the years Tom had known the banker he had never heard of him ever inviting anyone to his house. But, Tom reckoned, Jubal was just trying to be polite and sympathetic.

"I'll do that sometime," Tom said. Then he turned and walked out of the building. He didn't turn around but he could feel Jubal Johnson's eyes still on him as he stood under the shelter of the wooden overhang looking for Jack Madrid.

When Tom felt it was reasonable and natural he glanced over his shoulder but Jubal wasn't there. "You're letting your imagination run away with you," Tom said to himself.

Across the street Tom saw Jack talking to some cowhands who seemed to be doing more listening than jawing. Now and then one of them would nod or point out toward the open grassland. After a while they disbanded and Jack saw Tom and ambled slowly over to the bank.

Jack didn't reveal anything in his eyes. He stood beside Tom for a few moments before speaking.

"Talk around town is that Rune Ballard might have had something to do with this."

"Rune Ballard!" Tom sucked in air. "What would he have to do with it? He's nothing but a braggin' hotwind."

Jack shrugged.

"Like I said it was just talk. Those cowhands hang out at the Black Deuces and talk is pretty cheap there. Maybe there is something to it, maybe not."

"It's a start," Tom said. "Where does Rune hang out these days? Still in that shack south of town?"

Jack nodded. "Far as I know that's where he's at. Maybe we should take a little ride out there."

"Just what I was thinking."

They had to delay the ride since at that moment Ben Yoder saw them and came over to where they were standing.

"How's it going, Tom?"

Tom just nodded his head.

"In town on business?"

"That's right."

"Been seeing you around, Jack. A while ago you were jawing with some waddies. Any particular reason?"

Jack looked as innocent as a two-minute-old lamb. "Any harm in just passing the day?"

"If that was what you were doing. I guess I got a suspicious mind. Comes from wearing this badge. All kinds of ideas come into my head."

Tom didn't like the way Ben was talking. Only this wasn't the time to play it any way but ignorant. "That's what you get when you are a lawman. Guess it goes with the territory."

"Guess so."

Jack took a chunk off a plug of tobacco and munched on it. A brown dribble snuck out of the corner of his mouth and snaked down his grizzled jaw.

"You aiming on doing some bankin', Ben?"

Jack finally said. There was a faint light chocolate foam around his lips.

"I leave that to the money-grubbing ranchers," Ben replied and a quick smile told the two men that it was just a joke.

"I thought you lawmen earned more than day money," Jack said. "What with those rewards you split with bounty hunters."

"Don't know who you been talking to," Ben answered. "Or if you been getting too much prairie wind in your bonnet. It don't work that way, leastwise not with this drover."

After a while Tom thought that he and Jack had managed to persuade Ben they were just in town to transact some business and that was all.

"Drop in for coffee any time you're in town, you hear," Ben said as he headed back to the marshal's office.

When he was out of earshot Tom said, "I think we ought to pay a call on Rune Ballard."

"My thoughts exactly."

"We'll wait until Ben gets to his office and then we'll ride out of town like we were headed back to the ranch."

Jack understood and he kept a hawk-eye on Ben while he meandered down the boardwalk until he got to the jailhouse. When Ben opened the door and went inside Jack spit a wad of tobacco juice into the dusty street as a signal that it was all right for them to move onto their horses.

Some drovers had come into town and the attention they caused helped Tom and Jack to ride unnoticed down the street and out of Valiant.

Once they were free of the watchful eyes of Ben Yoder they spurred their horses and headed for Rune Ballard's place. Place was a kind word for the shack the grubby, no-account low-lifer lived in. It was a lean-to made from scrap wood and sparsely covered with flea-infested buffalo hides. The stench from the shack could be smelled two furlongs away. It was all they could do to keep from upchucking and Tom and Jack resisted the impulse to hold their noses.

Dismounting, Tom checked his six-gun and flicked it back into the holster. Madrid eased his long bladed knife from its scabbard and then slowly slipped it back. With someone like Rune Ballard these precautions were a necessity. It might make the difference between taking another breath after coming into contact with the man.

"Quiet, ain't it," Jack said.

"Too quiet."

They stood upwind of the shack hoping that the wind wouldn't change against them. A loose piece of buffalo hide, strung sloppily across the window, flapped and fluttered from a sudden gust of wind. Tom slapped his holster but didn't draw. Jack rubbed the ivory handle of his knife and his fingers drummed on the sheath.

"Can't stand here all day," Jack said.

"You're right. We're getting nowhere," Tom answered. He moved slowly toward what passed for a door to the shack. Both Tom and Madrid were alert for any sign of movement at the windows or from the doorway. Rune Ballard was as bad as they came. He wouldn't be above gunning a man in the back and then laughing about how he had tricked the man.

Tom reached out and with one quick thrust of his hand flung the door open. "Come on out, Ballard. We want to talk to you."

By this time Tom had his weapon out. He didn't want to come up the loser in this confrontation. Rune had quite an arsenal of weapons inside. Although Tom had never been inside the shack, he had talked to layabouts who had.

There was no answer. If Rune Ballard was inside he was being as quiet as a packrat on moving day.

Tom called out again. Then he turned to Jack. He made a motion with his head that said for Jack to get ready, they were going inside.

Taking a deep breath, not only from excitement but because of the overpowering odor that came from the shack, the two men cautiously entered the lean-to.

It was midnight dark inside. The only light came from a torn section of buffalo hide that dangled loosely from the window.

Tom moved about the one-room shack cautiously. If Rune Ballard was in there, which he very much doubted, he wouldn't be caught off-guard. There was no place for the hired gunslinger to hide so Tom and Jack made quick work of their search.

"He's not here," Jack said needlessly. "Let's get out of this place. It makes my flesh crawl."

"Don't know how the drover lives here."

"Knowing what I do of Rune Ballard, this place suits him like a kid glove. Don't he know what a bar of soap is for?"

They stumbled outside and filled their lungs with clear, clean air. It took them a few minutes to get over the stench of the shanty. Even their horses had turned their backsides so they faced the leeward side of the prairie.

"Wonder where he's at?" Tom asked, slipping his six-gun back into the holster. "What did they say about Rune in town?"

Jack sent a thin line of tobacco into the air. "Just that he had been boasting about coming into a little money. Since Rune never did an honest day's labor in his life, two and two were adding up to four."

"Ben Yoder said that nothing was taken, that he knew of, from the stagecoach. The strongbox wasn't even touched. So where did he come up with the money? If Rune is the man we're after."

"Dunno. But he ain't here. That's for sure."

"Still wonder where he's off to."

"With Rune Ballard there's no telling. He's a drifter. Surprised he's lasted this long in Valiant."

None of this was fresh news to Tom. He'd had his eye on Rune Ballard ever since he'd come to the valley over two years ago. From the first day he laid eyes on the man he knew he was a no-account. Just trouble in a pair of scuffed, run-down boots. He had had a few brushes with Marshal Yoder when he'd taken one too many shotglasses of rot-gut and had gone loco. Once he had broken all the windows out of the Wild Drover bar and had been in jail for a month because of that fracas. For Rune Ballard that was like going home for a vacation. Three squares a day and no bath to take and a roof over his scabby head.

"Ben Yoder told me he was glad to get rid of the drifter," someone had once remarked to Tom after Rune had been let out of jail. "Now he has to fumigate the whole jail."

That might have been stretching it a little but

after being in the shanty Tom was beginning to think the man hadn't exaggerated.

"Wonder where he's gone to?" Jack said it this time.

"No use staying around here. Let's ride back to the ranch."

They were about to lift themselves into their saddles when Ben Yoder rode up.

"Howdy, Ben, fancy seeing you again today." Jack's manner was matter-of-fact.

"What are you two doing here? Don't be telling me that you are good friends of Rune Ballard."

Tom slipped his boot into the stirrup and slowly eased his bad leg over the saddle.

"Just making a social call, Ben," Tom said. "Wondered if everything we heard about Rune was true."

"That he lived in a pigsty and was about as clean as a trail-dusted cowpoke," Jack said. "And everything we heard was true."

Ben leaned on the pommel of his saddle. "Don't believe either one of you."

"Your privilege, Ben," Tom said letting the reins go slack in his hands. "You wouldn't by any chance be following Jack and me."

For the first time Ben appeared to be a little uncertain. He was always in charge of every situation. Now, Tom figured, he had hit where it hurt.

"Nothing more than a coincidence me coming out here," Ben said. Then he made a grunting sound deep in his throat and said, "No, that isn't true. I came out here same as you. Wanted to ask Rune a question or two."

"We'll save you time," Tom said. "He's not in there. We checked."

Ben sat up straighter. "Any idea where he might have lit out to?"

Both Tom and Jack shook their heads.

"I guess I can level with you, Tom." Ben reached inside his vest pocket and pulled out the spent cartridges he had found at Devil's Whip. He opened his hand and the sunlight glinted on the shell casings.

"These I found up on Devil's Whip," Ben said. "Up the road from where the stagecoach went off. They were close to an outcropping of rocks. The ambusher must have been hiding there waiting for the stagecoach to come by."

Tom was very quiet but alert. This was the first time Ben had actually spoken to him about any evidence he might have found connected to the ambush and the murders.

"Do you think they came from one of Ballard's guns?" Tom asked.

"They might have. Can't think of anybody in

these parts who has as many firearms as Ballard has. Don't know how he came by so many."

Jack spit out a wad of tobacco. "Wasn't that he paid out money. He probably stole most of them."

Neither Ben Yoder nor Tom Cardy would offer any objections to that.

"So you think Ballard did the shooting?" Tom asked, staring straight at Ben.

"Now hold on, Tom. Nothing's been proven. I'm just doing some checking. Don't get any crazy ideas about stringing Rune up or something like that."

Tom just stared at the marshal.

"All I want to do is ask him some questions. Any harm in that?"

"Speech is free," Jack said as he got on his horse. "Leastwise that's what I've always been told."

"Depends on what you do with it." Ben's back got even more rigid. He was watching Tom to see if he could read his thoughts. After all these years he thought he knew Tom Cardy inside and out. That was before he got married to Caroline and lost her. Right now he wasn't sure he knew what Tom was thinking and it bothered him to no end.

"Look, Tom," Ben finally said. "When this is

all over what say you and I take a trip, do some hunting, like we used to do. What say?"

It wasn't the right thing to say to Tom, not at this moment. Ben realized that just as soon as the words had gone out of his mouth. It made Caroline and the rest of the passengers' deaths seem not all that important. And that wasn't what he had intended, not at all.

"Forget it. I didn't mean that," Ben added. He knew he had overstepped the bounds of friendship and it was time he drew in his hand and moved out.

"But that offer for coffee still goes," Ben said as he took the reins into his powerful hands. "You included, Jack."

"Much obliged, Ben," Jack said and he moved his body in the saddle.

"Thanks, Ben," was all that Tom said. It was enough to let Ben know that there were no hard feelings and that he might have said the wrong thing, but everyone had their days.

Ben snapped the reins and his red roan gelding galloped away. Neither Jack nor Tom said anything about Ben when he was gone. But it was Jack who asked, "Do you think those shells came from one of Ballard's rifles? Didn't git that close a gander but they looked to me to be rifle cartridges."

"For now I guess we'll just have to wait until

Ballard gets back from wherever it is he's gone to. He couldn't have gone very far, he still had some belongings in there."

Jack sniffed. "Such as they were."

"He could be a lot neater," Tom said and they both chuckled at that. It had been a long time since Tom had laughed or even grinned for that matter. But it was over in a snapped finger and he grew somber once again. This was no time for him to be jollying around what with Caroline only buried a day before.

"Where to now?" Jack asked, growing somber like Tom.

"Back home," Tom said. "For now, anyway."

Jack's grey pinto was anxious to get moving. "And then?"

"I think we ought to take a look see at Devil's Whip."

Chapter Four

Tom had taken on some temporary help around the ranch. Actually they were the two oldest sons of Andre Dusault. He needed them to ride herd on his cattle while he and Jack went about the business of finding Caroline's killer.

After the boys had decided, when if need be, who would take the drag and would ride on point, Tom felt that the ranch and the grazing range were in good hands. So he and Jack set out for Devil's Whip. It was early morning when they left the ranch.

There was the scent of winter in the air and this early in the day their breaths billowed out from their mouths like vaporous garlands.

"What you aimin' on finding at Devil's Whip

41

that Ben Yoder hasn't already?" Jack asked when they had gone a few miles from the ranch.

"Don't know. One thing is I just got to see where it happened. The coach is still there. They won't get it out until spring."

"You sure you want to do this, Tom?"

"I got to, Jack. If you don't want to make the ride I'll understand."

"You'll understand nothing," Jack replied in a low voice. "I'm in this the same as you, Tom Cardy. Don't you commence trying to figure out my motives."

Tom didn't take this as a dressing down. He just nodded to Jack in understanding. The two had only been friends for a couple of years. It wasn't the same brother-to-brother relationship he shared with Ben Yoder. Still, Jack was reliable and handy with a six-gun or a knife. Tom didn't ask what Jack's background was. You just didn't do that out here in the wilds of Wyoming. You just studied a man for a length of time and made your choice whether he was on the up-and-up or not. If you made a mistake in your judgement then it was your bad luck.

Ahead of them rose the mountain range where Devil's Whip ran its deadly course. Tom was familiar with this part of the land since he and Ben Yoder had ridden it many times in their youth. Sometimes they went hunting, sometimes they just wanted to get away from Valiant and all their problems. Either way when they trotted their horses along the deadly ridge of the Whip, they forgot everything but trying to keep their horses from bolting and going over the side.

"Where you think Rune Ballard got to?" Jack said, making conversation.

"Cheyenne maybe," Tom said. "I've heard he goes there sometimes."

"Cheyenne's a good town," Jack replied. "Got real close to settling down there once."

Tom glanced under the brim of his Stetson at Jack. This was the first time the grizzled drover had ever spoken of his past. As far as Tom was concerned Jack had no past. He had just suddenly appeared one day, free as a prairie wind, in Valiant.

"Need a good woman to settle down," Tom said.

"Found one," was Jack's answer. "At least I thought I had. Didn't turn out that way."

That was about as much as Jack decided to reveal of his past that day, so Tom accepted the brief entry into Jack Madrid's past life and shifted in his saddle. His leg still bothered him slightly, if he sat in the wrong position. The doctor in town had said it would be another couple of weeks before it was healed completely. In the meantime Tom was to favor it. But that was before news of Caroline's death had reached Valiant.

"That banker feller, what's his name?" Jack said about a half-hour later.

"Johnson. Jubal Johnson. Why you bringing him up?"

"No reason. Just saw him watching you out the window the other day when we was in town."

"I kinda thought he was. Guess he was just being sympathetic."

Jack leaned on his pommel. "What's his story? Know anything about him?"

"Just what he wants people to know. Hails from back East. His ma and two sisters died from a diptheria plague. Never mentions his pa but I heard he had two brothers die in the War. Johnson never married but came out here and found a job at the bank."

Jack was listening as he bit off a wad of tobacco. "He must be a smart one."

"Hear tell. Started as a teller and in a couple of years was manager. His ma was a social person back East and she taught him reading and ciphering."

"Ciphering's probably what got him the job at the bank. What's this about him having a place in town that's like a library?"

Tom was only speaking from hearsay and

didn't know if he should elaborate on Jubal Johnson's home.

"Don't know if it's what you would call a library, since I never been there myself. I did hear some folks in town saying as how he did have a passel of books in there."

Tom didn't want to be reminded of books since that had been Caroline's passion. She loved to read to herself and read to Tom. If he didn't stop thinking of Caroline he would burst like a cotton ball. So Tom directed his thoughts to the trail that was beginning to spread upwards where the mountains stood.

Tom and Madrid were in the low foothills now. Around them stood aspens with their shivering, silver-splattered leaves. Then there were poplars with their yellow, fading ones. A stream edged the trail and the bone-chilling pure water gurgled over glistening pebbles and stones. If it had been another time, another mission, Tom would have thought everything was eye-fillingly beautiful. But he had no time for that now. He and Jack had to keep alert for the turnoff that led to the mountains and to Devil's Whip.

It was Jack who first spotted the two horsemen as they rode out from behind a stand of aspens. They were both on chestnuts and their battered felt hats hugged their heads and cast their faces in deep shadows.

"What we got coming on?" Jack said and his hand went automatically to his holster, where it lingered with his fingers drumming on the leather covering.

"Don't recollect ever seeing either of them before," was Tom's reply.

As the two riders got nearer Tom could make out their features more clearly. One was older than the other, but not by much. There was a strong family resemblance between the two of them and Tom felt that he had seen them somewhere before. The older man appeared to be about Tom's age. The other one had an impudent, chip-on-the-shoulder look that spelled trouble wherever he went.

When they were about face to face with Tom and Jack, the older man held up a hand in greeting. Tom did the same.

"Can you tell us if we're on the right road to Valiant?" the older man asked. The younger man, obviously his brother, kept a watchful eye on Madrid and he seemed to be sizing him up for a call. Then, when he got a little closer and got a real good look at the grizzled, seasoned Jack Madrid, he changed his mind real quick.

"Back yonder," Tom said. "You can't miss it."

"Much obliged," the older man said.

"Got business in Valiant?" Jack surprisingly said.

"Maybe," was the younger brother's reply. "Any harm in that?"

Jack just gave the boy a curt smile.

"None of my business what you do."

"C'mon, there," the older man said. "We're wasting valuable time jawing."

The younger brother, Wes, kept a wary eye on Jack as they rode away. He glanced once over his shoulder when they were enough furlongs away so that he didn't have a direct confrontation.

"Wonder what they are up to?" Tom asked.

"Don't know," was Jack's response. "But that kid is headed for a sackful of trouble. He's got bad written all over him."

"I noticed the way he was sizing you up," Tom said. "Only I think he knew he would be biting off more than he could chew."

"Still got his baby teeth," chuckled Jack.

"Let's get a move on," Tom said. "We still got a ways to go before we get to Devil's Whip."

The two brothers were quickly forgotten as Tom and Jack galloped their horses toward the mountains. It had turned colder as they began to climb to the heights of the foothills. Here and there were splotches of white from an early snow-fall. The breathing of their horses became more labored and the vapor from their breath was almost palpable and alive.

Every once in a while Tom would glance over

his shoulder. It was a habit he had picked up from riding alone for so many years. He halfway expected to see Marshal Ben Yoder shagging up the hill behind them. Ben wasn't anybody's fool. He had put a few things together, Tom was certain, after he had found Jack and himself at Rune Ballard's shack. He had warned them not to interfere but, on the other hand, he knew Tom's nature, Tom's dogged way to get to answers on problems. He knew that Tom wouldn't let things just lie, he was a man of action and he couldn't wait for the law to come to follow its course.

Reaching the end of the foothills, they decided to give their horses a breather. After tethering them to some shrubs, Tom and Jack found two smooth-surfaced rocks and sat down. Jack bit into his plug of tobacco, offered Tom a chew, and was refused.

"We come a long way in a short time," Jack said, aiming a wad of tobacco juice at a weathered piece of bark. "Where is this Devil's Whip?"

"See that stand of pine, way up yonder?" Tom pointed. Jack squinted and then nodded. "That's the end of the Whip. Lot of bad road up there. Got to be real careful where you put your boot or you'll be spitting sandstone for a week or worse."

Jack noticed that Tom was choosing his words carefully. He didn't want to make any reference to Caroline's death. His grieving was still going on but he was coping with it real well.

"You give much thought to the future, Tom?" Jack asked, folding his arms across his chest. He didn't look at Tom when he said this, just stared down at the long valley.

"Enough to just think about today," was Tom's answer. "What you getting at?"

"Nothing, really. Just wondering if you aim on keeping the ranch and the cattle."

Tom looked at Jack, surprised. He hadn't expected these words to come from the man.

" 'Course I'm going to keep the ranch and I'm still in the cattle business. This spread was mine and Caroline's. We put a lot of hard work and hours into it. It's ours, hers and mine."

"Only askin'," Jack replied. "Thought you might sometime in the future think of pullin' stakes and going someplace else."

Tom shook his head.

"Valiant's my home, Jack. It's where I was reared. Can't think of anyplace else I'd rather live. Is that the answer you were wanting?"

"Pretty close. None of my business, really. Think we better be heading out?"

"Let's move," said Tom and they untied the reins and lifted themselves into their saddles.

Within an hour they had reached Devil's Whip. It was just as Tom had remembered: twisting, serpentine, and just as deadly dangerous as a rattle-snake. Now that they were there Jack recognized the road. He had been on it before and he knew how treacherous it could be.

They formed a single-file pace with Jack following Tom. The road was wide enough to accommodate both horses but if they happened to meet a coach or wagon with a team of six horses it would be easier for them to get out of the way.

Tom and Jack made a silent pair as their horses clomped along near the edge of the road. Tom was eagerly searching the slope of the mountainside for the first trace of the murder scene.

It was midway down the road toward what some people called the handle of the Whip that the two horsemen reined in their horses.

"Down there," Tom said and nodded his head so that Jack could see where he was looking. The coach still lay impaled on the huge boulder that had claimed the lives of the passengers.

"Looks like the wolves have had a feed," Jack said as he beheld the grisly sight of the horses—or what was left of them. It was a sickening sight and both men lifted their kerchiefs to cover their noses which did very little to alleviate the stench.

After they had taken care of their horses, Tom and Jack scampered down the side of the mountain, being careful to latch onto any outgrowth so they wouldn't lose their footing and plummet down the sandstone cliff.

Tom gingerly made his way to the overturned stagecoach. One of the doors had been ripped from its hinges by the bone-jolting crash against the mammoth boulder. He peered inside and could see clearly by the light cast by the near-winter sunshine. It was empty, except for a shoe that lay in one corner and a thin layer of sand that had settled lightly on the seats of the coach.

It was too risky for him to try and climb aboard the coach. But he had seen what he wanted to see and hadn't found what he had been looking for. Jack came up silently beside him.

"Seen enough?" was all he said.

"She might have been sitting right there. By that window. All I can hope is that she didn't suffer any."

"From what I heard none of them did. It happened so darn quick they probably didn't know what hit them."

That should have assuaged Tom some but it didn't. How did anyone know the way Caroline had died? They weren't there. All the scene of carnage did was to renew Tom's secret vow for revenge.

"Let's go. I've seen enough," Tom finally said.

Side by side they climbed slowly back up the steep face of the cliff to their horses. They had just swung their feet over their saddles and into the stirrups when a barrage of bullets pinged around them, kicking up dust and spooking the horses. Tom's black mustang reared onto its back legs and almost threw its ride from the saddle. Tom held on tightly and when the mustang had landed on its front legs urged it across the road and into the safety of an overhanging ledge. Jack had been right behind him.

Once under the ledge both men leaped from their saddles and their six-guns were in their hands before their feet touched the ground.

"Did you see where they came from?" Jack asked, peering out from behind a boulder.

"Somewhere up there," Tom answered just as another burst of bullets twanged the earth around them and ricocheted off the small rocks that were strewn around them.

"I'm getting off some fire," Jack said. "I'm not just going to stand here and be a damned target."

Jack fell to the ground and rolled away from the cliff and fanned the trigger of his gun when he stopped and then rolled back again. This action must have taken the shooter by surprise because Jack was safely back under the shelter of the cliff before a volley of bullets ripped through the air and sent up splinters of rock in quick, stinging showers.

Before the burst of gunfire had ceased Tom

leaned out and emptied his Colt against the unseen enemy. After that there was a stillness that was even worse than the hail of bullets. So quiet you could hear the wind whining up the narrow twisting road. It was spooky and a shiver went down Jack's back.

"Come on you skunk-bellied coward!" Jack shouted in anger. "Show yourself. Or are you too chicken to meet a man face to face?"

The stillness was even more pronounced. The horses had settled down and were nibbling on whatever late blooming fodder grew alongside the road. This was an indication to Tom that whoever had taken potshots at them might have gone.

"He's not there anymore," Tom said.

"It could be a trick. He might still be there trying to fool us into showing ourselves."

Tom had to agree with Madrid. It would be foolhardy of them not to wait. The shooter might just be crafty and kill-hungry enough to have the patience to wait them out. Tom and Jack waited. Time dragged on and on. Jack even went so far as to pull out his plug tobacco and take a chew.

"Let's try something," Tom said. "We can't be pinned down here all day."

He looked around and found a dead, withered branch of a pine tree. Tom picked it up and tossed it out beyond where they were hiding. He braced himself for a volley of shots, but none came.

Tom looked at Jack. "Want to chance it?"

"If we don't we could be here all day and night."

So they got on their horses and on a nod from Tom, spurred the animals and bolted out from the protection of the overhanging cliff and back down Devil's Whip. Tom hunkered his body in anticipation of some shots that could be fired. He needn't have worried—the shooter had long since departed the Whip and the mountain itself.

Not caring about the danger of falling from the Whip, the two men urged their horses on, sometimes narrowly missing a turn and the possibility of toppling to a sure death on the jagged rocks below.

By the time they reached the foothills their horses were wheezing and breathing with labored breaths. Tom and Jack allowed the horses to slow to a leisurely trot and they both turned in their saddles to look back at the mountain.

"He's long gone by now," Jack said. "He probably hightailed it out of there when the shooting first stopped."

"I'm thinking it was the same person who shot Gordy and Red. Wonder why he wanted to kill us?"

"Maybe not kill us, just put a scare in us."

"But what?"

Tom shook his head.

"Wonder who it could have been?" Jack shifted in the saddle so that he could look at Tom. "You having the same thoughts I am?"

"If you mean Rune Ballard, you're right."

"Only thing is Rune wasn't at his place when we were there. How did he know we would be coming up to Devil's Whip?"

Tom shrugged.

"He might have been there already. We could have just come along and he decided to have a little fun."

"Sounds like Rune Ballard, all right."

Tom thought about Rune Ballard and the possibility that he was the gunslinger all the way back to Valiant. He didn't know but Jack Madrid was thinking along the same lines. Jack not only thought Rune Ballard was the shooter but that he would like to reciprocate and feed Ballard a few cartridges from his own six-shooter.

It was getting on toward dusk when they rode into Valiant. From the distance they could see lights from oil lamps blazing in the storefront windows. On the outskirts of town women were calling in their menfolk and children for supper.

It should have been a warm, mellow scene but it was hurtful to Tom. At times like these the memory of Caroline came back to Tom in painful melancholy images.

Jack sensed Tom's mood and attempted to distract him.

"How about some grub, Tom? I'm as hungry as a winter-starved grizzly."

"Sounds good to me. We can grab a bite to eat at The Busted Nugget. Hear they got a new cook."

" 'Bout time. That last cook could burn water."

They ambled down the main street of Valiant until they came to The Busted Nugget. There were a few horses tethered to the hitchrail and Tom thought he recognized two of the chestnut geldings that were standing there.

"Looks like our friends from the trail are hungry too," Jack said.

"I got a feeling we're going to get more than supper when we go in there," were Tom's words as they crossed the boardwalk and entered through the batwing doors.

The Busted Nugget was more of a saloon than an eatery. There was the usual layer of blue smoke drifting over the heads of the few men who were seated at the tables eating supper or drinking rot-gut whiskey. It wasn't hard to find a table so Tom and Jack took one not far from the doors.

Big Bert Conley came over to their table. He had a greasy apron strapped around his wide gut and his muscular arms strained at the flannel shirt he wore. His black, bushy mustache was flecked with white hairs.

"Hi, Tom, sorry to hear about your wife," the owner of The Busted Nugget said in his direct, brusque way. "Howdy, Jack. Two beers?"

"Okay by me," Tom said and Jack just nodded in agreement. "Hear you got a new cook. Any good?"

"As long as I keep him off the white lightning," Big Bert answered in his rough-as-a-corncob voice. "You want something to eat too?"

"What's on special?" Jack asked.

"Steak and taters. All we got."

That met with an all-around agreement by the two men. Big Bert Conley went away to bring their beers and give the order to the new cook.

After Big Bert had gone, Tom and Madrid hung their hats on the posts of an empty chair. Across the room they heard a commotion. It didn't come as any great surprise when they saw it was the younger brother of the two riders they had met earlier on the trail to Devil's Whip.

"That pup is just itchin' for a fight," Jack said. "And in here that itch'll git some good scratchin'."

The older brother was sitting quietly, one hand on his shot glass of rot-gut. His brother, whose name was Wes, Wesley Taylor, Tom later learned, was going on about how somebody would have to pay, pay real good for what happened to his brother.

The older brother, Slim, who lived up to his moniker, thin and wiry as a railroad tie, waved a hand at him to tone it down.

"Hell, I don't have to shut up," Wes said. "Anybody here think they're man enough to make me just step forward."

It so happened at that moment Mokey Stewart unfortunately staggered by their table. Mokey was a harmless drunk, about the size of a spavined monkey, and he did odd jobs around town to keep himself in liquor. Mokey was none too steady on his feet in ordinary times but when he had a snoot-full he was downright clumsy.

Mokey accidentally bumped Wes's drinking arm and the younger brother leaped to his feet and backhanded Mokey, sending him sprawling across the room. Blood gushed out of the fragile, little man's mouth and he was out cold. Wes walked over and laughed at the sight of Mokey bleeding. Then he reached down and picked up a spittoon and poured its putrid contents all over his sprawled body.

This last indignity was too much for Jack. He was on his feet and sprinted over to where Mokey lay. "How about someone who can defend himself, you outhouse slime," Jack said and he smashed Wes's jaw with his fist and sent him tumbling backwards over the table.

Even as much as his jaw must have been hurting him Wes staggered to his feet and took a wide, wild swing at Jack. Jack easily moved aside and shoved Wes with one hand and the younger brother of Slim Taylor hit the floor, raw flesh splashing blood over everything.

Tom was on his feet watching this and so he saw Slim reach across the table for the whiskey bottle and ease himself to his feet. He raised his arm to smash the bottle on Madrid's head but he never got the chance.

Tom grabbed Slim's arm and twisted it with such force he heard a snapping, cracking sound from his shoulder joint. Slim cried out in pain and tried to reach for his gun with his good hand. Tom was prepared for that and he lashed out with a well-aimed kick to Slim's groin. The older Taylor brother collapsed with a painful scream next to his younger brother.

"That'll be enough," came a voice from the doorway. Both Tom and Jack turned to look in that direction. There stood Marshal Ben Yoder with his Colt drawn and at the ready. He meant business and the steady, level aiming of his gun attested to that.

Chapter Five

"Tom and Jack, they didn't start it," Big Bert said, wiping his hands on the grimy apron. "These two crazy drovers came in begging for a fight. Look what they done to poor Mokey."

By this time Mokey had come around. He sat up looking dazed and bewildered. He wiped the blood from his mouth with the back of his hand then said, "I need another drink."

Big Bert picked Mokey up and sat him at a table. He held his nose with two fingers and said, "What you need is a good bath and a scrubbin' with lye soap."

Mokey visibly shivered at this suggestion. "Only if you promise me a drink when I'm finished."

60

Slim Taylor had recovered enough to get to his feet, and he then helped Wes to a rather unsteady, weaving posture.

"What do you two have to say for yourselves?" Ben Yoder asked as he moved toward the center of the saloon. "I saw you ride into town this afternoon. Just what is your business here in Valiant?"

Wes was too out of it to speak so Slim became the voice for the Taylor brothers.

"Wes and me came here to claim our brother's body," Slim said and rubbed his sore arm. "Now I think I need to see a doc. You got one in this town?"

"Body? Where is your brother's body? And who is your brother?" Ben asked.

Wes had to sit down. He held his head in his hands and there was a faint moaning sound coming from somewhere deep inside him.

"Frank is our brother. We saw him over at the funeral parlor."

"Was he one of the folks got killed on the stagecoach?" Big Bert asked.

"He was coming back from Denver. Got into a ruckus over there. Had his head bandaged up."

"So that man's name is Frank Taylor," Ben said. "Only leaves us two we haven't got names to. What you need a doc for?"

"My arm," Slim said. "I think it's broken."

"We'll get you a doc," Ben Yoder said. "Any ideas who might have killed your brother and the rest of the passengers?"

Slim's mouth twisted in a mocking grin. "Sure Wes and me got an idea. It had to be George Gadsen. He was gettin' even with Frank for stealing his gal."

"Let's go over to my office," Ben said. "We'll go over all this. No use spouting off here in a saloon."

"Hold the steaks, Big Bert," Jack said.

"We'll be back in a while," Tom said. "Unless we're arrested for disturbing the peace."

Ben Yoder wasn't smiling. "I haven't decided on that yet."

"I'll have the steak and taters ready when you two get back," Big Bert said. "If you're in jail I'll bring it over to you."

Ben let Tom and Jack gather up their hats and then all five of them left The Busted Nugget. Tom was dusty, hungry, and so heated up over the fight that he wasn't tired. He wanted to learn more about this Frank Taylor and who George Gadsen was. Maybe this was the answer he had been seeking ever since Caroline had been killed.

The five of them were so quiet going to the jailhouse you would have thought they were headed for a funeral. Quiet except for Wes Taylor who kept up a low, keening moan like some kind of wounded animal. Tom would have felt sorry for him had it not been for the way he had treated Mokey Stewart. It took a beating for some men to learn they didn't own the earth. Tonight Wes Taylor had taken a step toward maturity.

Jack Madrid had no such thoughts as he moved along the boardwalk beside Tom. He was hungry and agitated. These two drovers had done him out of a good, hot meal and he resented them. Even if they were in Valiant to claim their brother's body, they sure had a peculiar way of showing their grief. That young one, that was Wes Taylor, was headed for a real short life span. Arrogant bully—Jack couldn't stand the type. Jack grew up in a hurry in Arizona when he was left an orphan at the age of twelve, and had had to fight to stay alive in the streets of Tucson. He had never been coddled or catered to in his life and couldn't understand a man who had been. A short life span, and a long stay in Boot Hill, that was where Wes Taylor was headed.

Slim Taylor was thinking about his dead younger brother, Frank, who was a year older than Wes, but still young to Slim. He had made a promise to his pa on his death bed he would make sure his two brothers stayed on this side of the law. With Wes it hadn't been easy, almost impossible. He was a headstrong hombre who did what he wanted to do regardless of the consequences and what wiser heads had told him not to do. Frank was the opposite. He was easygoing and likeable as a newborn colt. He never defended himself and was always being taken advantage of. He seldom fought back. Only time he did was when he had a few gut-warmers too many and then thought he could tackle the world. In that respect he was a lot like Wes. Only Wes was always hankering for a brawling fight.

Wes was just feeling hurt and numb. He didn't have a single thought in his brain, only feelings of revenge. He didn't like the thought of being bested by this no-account skunk who was walking behind him. Only right now he couldn't do anything about it. Oh, his mouth hurt!

At the jailhouse Ben sent for Doc Kreugger to mend the broken bones and stitch up any cut and torn flesh. Then he poured coffee all around.

"Sit down," he commanded. "I want to get to the bottom of all this."

Grudgingly the men took seats. Tom and Jack sat in one area and the two brothers sat opposite them. Ben was at his oaken desk.

"Where you men from?"

Wes looked to his brother Slim to answer the marshal.

"Over near Bad Falls, we got a spread of land with a hundred head of cattle. Me and Wes and my brother Frank run the place. Only we ain't got Frank anymore."

Slim took a sip of the steaming, strong coffee and looked around the room before he continued.

"Frank met this gal, Rosebelle, one night at a dance over in Bad Falls. They got along real well. What Frank didn't know was that George Gadsen also had tried to stake a claim on her. George had a bad temper and he and Frank got into it that night over Rosebelle. Frank may be meek as a sheep sometimes but when the right time comes he can be a Kansas twister."

Again Slim took in some coffee. The room was quiet as he unfolded the story of his brother and Rosebelle. Slim had a way of spinning a yarn that was spellbinding. Not so much what he said but the way he spoke—just the right emphasis on something suspenseful, and knowing when to pause for the maximum effect it had.

"Anyway, George came out second best in the fracas. He vowed he would get even with Frank one way or another. Guess he did."

"Are you telling us that this Gadsen feller was the shooter up there on Devil's Whip?" Ben Yoder asked.

"That's my opinion," Slim said. "You don't know George Gadsen. He's mean as a scalded wildcat."

Wes finally spoke. "Slim's right. He's the one

that killed my brother. George caused that accident, if you want to call it that."

"You men got any proof?" Tom couldn't hold on any longer.

"We can get it," Slim said.

"Damn right we can," Wes said. "What's it to you anyway?"

Ben Yoder spoke up. "Tom's wife was killed when that stagecoach went off the trail. He's got more than just a casual interest in this."

"Sorry," Slim said and he genuinely did seem to be. His younger brother didn't seem to care one way or the other, which didn't surprise Jack Madrid any. "We didn't know that."

"You mean this Gadsen feller would try and make a stagecoach go over the cliff to kill a rival? That's kind of hard to swallow," Ben said.

Doc Kreugger came in then and took a long look at the two men.

"Another barroom brawl?" the doc said as he looked first at Wes's face and then, not too gently, worked on Slim's arm.

"Keeps you in business, Doc," Jack said and then drained the last of his coffee.

"I got plenty of business, thank you, without you men adding to it. Hold still." Doc Kreugger snapped Slim's arm back in place and the skinny cowboy passed out, hitting the floor with a crunching, soft thud. "He'll come around in a minute or two. The rest will do him good."

"You quack! That's my brother." Wes was about to move on the doctor but, seeing how outnumbered he was, changed his mind.

Doc Kreugger put some ointment on Wes's face and you could tell by the tears in Wes's eyes that it hurt like anything. "That should take care of you."

The doctor looked around and asked, "Anyone else? Must have been a quiet night at the Nugget."

Ben told the doctor that he should stop by the saloon and check on Mokey Stewart. "He got a pretty bad one in the mouth."

After the doctor had gone and Slim came around, Ben said, "You were talkin' about the Gadsen hombre. How he might cause a stagecoach to go over at Devil's Whip because of a gal?"

Slim nodded. The doctor had put his arm in a makeshift sling and the hand from that arm dangled helplessly from the mouth of the sling. "That's right. No might about it, Marshal. George Gadsen is really loco. He doesn't reason like other men. And if you cross him there's no telling what that mind of his will think up.

"So far he's about the best I've heard of that I can pin this thing on."

"Then you think it's this Gadsen who killed Caroline, am I right, Ben?" Tom said.

Ben slowly nodded. "Looks that way."

"What are we waiting for?" Jack was on his feet. "Where can we find this drover?"

Ben held up his hand. "Not so fast. We, as you put it, aren't going to find Gadsen. It's up to the law to take care of him. None of this vigilante stuff."

Tom said, "We're going to Bad Falls, Ben. Ain't nothing you can do to stop us. Man's entitled to take a ride if he's of a mind. Right?"

"Wrong. I know what you're up to, Tom, and I won't allow it."

Slim got to his feet this time.

"While you two are at it, can Wes and me get Frank's body and take it home for a proper burial? Or are we under arrest, Marshal?"

"By rights I ought to look you two up," Ben said. "But considering the circumstance I'm letting you go. Only if you get into any more trouble before leaving Valiant I'm locking you up. Understand?"

Slim and Wes attested to how they understood. Then they went out of the office.

After they had gone Tom said, "Ben, I want to go find this Gadsen feller. You know how it is."

Ben allowed that he did. "There is a way that the three of us can go over to Bad Falls, nice and legal. I'm appointing you two my deputies. Right this minute I'm swearing you in. Do I hear any objections?"

None came from Tom or Jack.

"Now that we're deputies, when do we head for Bad Falls?" Jack asked with a slight twist of irony to his mouth.

"Tomorrow morning we slap leather," Ben replied. "Got a few things I want to get in order before we head north."

"Fair enough," Tom said. "How about that steak and taters, Jack? Big Bert told us he'd keep them hot for us."

"Ready when you are, Deputy."

Before they left Ben told them he would meet them at the ranch at sunrise.

When the sun split the sky the next morning the three men were in the saddle headed north. Ben was good as his word and arrived at the ranch on time. Tom was astride his mustang, Jack his pinto, and Ben rode his red roan gelding. Each had his Colt tucked on the ready in his holster. Tom had brought along some beans and jerky just in case they were gone longer than they had anticipated.

"Just one question, Marshal," Jack said, tying a knot in the kerchief around his neck.

"What may that be?" Ben said, turning to face Madrid.

"Any idea where we might find this hombre Gadsen?"

"After you men went to eat I had a little gab-fest with Slim and Wes at Josh Merkin's. It shouldn't be too hard to find Gadsen. He's always around town. Owns a mercantile store there."

"Good enough," Jack said, satisfied with the answer he got.

"Do you know what Gadsen looks like?" asked Tom, rubbing his healing leg with one hand.

"Slim said he was about six foot, had wide shoulders, brown hair that came down to his shoulders, and a perfect S scar down his left cheek."

Tom looked at his boyhood friend closely and then said, "Don't think we'll have any trouble locating that drover."

"When we do," Ben said. "we tackle him to-gether, understood? We bring him back to Valiant for trial. We don't want to make any mistakes here."

Jack nodded in agreement and slowly Tom managed a quick bob of his head. "I guess you're right, Marshal," Tom said with no emotion in his voice. "Let's don't make no mistakes."

"Slim said he hadn't seen Gadsen hanging around town for a while. That's another good rea-son to think he might be the shooter," Ben said, touching the walnut-handled butt of his Colt to make sure it rode easy.

By noon they could see the small town of Big Falls dead ahead. Tom reckoned they would be there in a half hour. He began to feel tense and the palms of his hands felt sweaty against the leather of the reins. Could it really be possible that he would soon confront the man responsible for Caroline's death? He wondered what he would do, what his first reaction would be. With Ben along he didn't dare draw on the man. Although if Ben got in the way, and this was the man they were seeking, friendship longstanding wouldn't come between him and retribution.

"What do you think would keep the Taylor boys from doing in Gadsen?" Jack asked and lifted a laconic eyebrow at Ben.

"Hadn't thought about that until now," Ben replied. There was an uneasiness in his voice and he seemed restless in the saddle.

"They just might take the law into their own hands," Tom said. "Especially that Wes. He's an ornery no-account."

"Maybe they've taken Frank to the undertaker's and are waiting for us to come into town. Slim just might have the good sense not to do anything foolish until we get there," Ben said, but his voice wasn't too reassuring.

Tom was silent the rest of the way to Bad

Falls; he didn't want to dwell on the fact that the
Taylor boys might take matters into their own
hands. He didn't want to admit to himself that
that was what he was intending on doing himself.
He was becoming more and more anxious to put
these miles to Bad Falls behind him. Madrid, he
knew, would go along with anything he intended
on doing. Now that they were deputized they
could make the whole thing appear perfectly legal.

When they got to Bad Falls they found a city
that was smaller than Valiant with dusty roads
and false-fronted buildings and boardwalks that
here and there had weeds poking through splin-
tered sections.

"Let's grab a bite to eat first," Ben said, notic-
ing a saloon that served food along with the liquid refreshment.

"Sounds good to me," Jack said, already off
his horse and tethering it to the hitchrail.

"Guess we got time," was all that Tom said.
He had been scrutinizing the town looking for the
mercantile store. That was where he knew they
would find George Gadsen.

Inside the saloon they had a beer and the cook
fixed them some fried chicken and grits. The barkeep put down their beers and Ben said, "You
know a man named George Gadsen? Runs the
mercantile hear tell."

The barkeep ran a practiced, professional eye over Ben and said, "You a lawman?"

"That's right."

"What you lookin' for George Gadsen for? If it's any of my business?"

"Your business is serving up whiskey," Jack said. "Our business is the law."

"Good enough," the barkeep said. "Don't want to stir up no trouble."

The barkeep started to walk away. Ben stopped him. "You didn't answer my question."

"I know George Gadsen. His place is just down the street. Across from the Wells Fargo. Any more questions?"

"Much obliged to you," Ben said. The barkeep went away. He didn't seem to be riled by the conversation. To him it was just another day's business.

"If Gadsen is our man," Tom said, "can we just walk into that store and arrest him?"

Ben shook his head. "I'll have to check with the local marshal before I do that. It is his territory. I'd want the same courtesy if he was lookin' for a man over at Valiant."

When the cook brought them their chicken Jack said, "You ever meet an hombre named Gadsen?"

"Maybe. Just about everyone comes in here

sooner or later." He put the platter of fried chicken down on the table.

"Gadsen," Ben said. "Owns the local mercantile."

The cook, whose face was lined with thin, red, blood vessels and who had a shining, bulbous nose, thought for a minute and then said, "Oh, yeah. He used to come in here real regular. Always caused some kind of ruckus or another. Just sowin' his wild oats I reckon."

Tom jabbed a piece of chicken with his fork and put it on his plate.

"Tall fella, had a scar on his face. Said he got that in a fight in a saloon over in Cheyenne. Wouldn't doubt that he lost the fight. More of a big mouth than a fighter."

"You seem him in here lately?" Tom wanted to know. "You seen him in here maybe in the last few days?"

"Don't recollect I have," the cook said, scratching his head. " 'Course I'm back in the kitchen a lot. Don't see everybody that comes in here unless they order up something."

"Well, obliged for the information," Ben said and he laddled some grits on his plate along with some chicken.

"Just sowin' his oats, huh," Jack said after he had taken a bite of the chicken.

"Sounds like he's been sowin' more than that," Ben said. "If he's the man we're after."

"We'll see," Tom said, only he had a gut feeling something wasn't quite right. That was confirmed when the cook came back out from the kitchen wiping his hands on a dingy-looking towel.

"One other thing about this Gadsen fella. Here tell he got hitched up a few days ago." Then he chuckled. "Maybe that's why nobody's been seein' much of him lately."

Chapter Six

It was like being hit by a charging bull buffalo. Tom shifted his steady gaze from the cook to Jack Madrid to Ben Yoder.

"Did I say something wrong?" the cook said, his nostrils widening and closing like a pair of bellows.

"No, you did fine," Ben said, not trying to disguise the disappointment in his voice. "This chicken is real fine eatin'."

The cook broke into a jagged-tooth grin and headed back to the kitchen. He had no idea of the disappointing news he had just handed the three men.

"So George Gadsen was married a few days ago," Tom said, the taste of the chicken turning sour in his mouth. "That cancels him out as a suspect."

"Hold on now," said Ben. "We still got to check on him. Maybe the cook got him mixed up. Maybe he didn't get married at all."

"Lots of maybes there, Marshal," Jack said and reached for another helping of grits.

"It's all right, Jack," Tom said. "Ben's right. We gotta follow this thing clean through."

"You said it," Jack said.

They took their time finishing up the chicken and grits. Tom was still debating in his mind whether this Gadsen was guilty or not. It seemed almost too easy, their coming here to Bad Falls expecting to tie the whole thing up in a neat little bundle.

They left their horses tethered at the hitchrail while they walked to the mercantile store. It was just a block from where they had eaten, just as they had been told.

The store was almost empty that time of the day. An older woman, gray-haired and with sharp, almost chiseled features was behind the counter and eyed them suspiciously when they entered.

"What can I do for you gentlemen?" she asked in a voice that was almost as sharp and chiseled as her features.

Ben stepped forward. The sunlight coming in

from the storefront window glistened on his badge. Immediately the woman's attitude changed. She became coy and almost shy in manner when she spoke next.

"I didn't know you were an officer of the law, Marshal. We all respect the law here in Bad Falls. Our marshal is a fine, upstanding man and we have two churches that are being built. A Methodist and a Congregational. Never did like that name, Bad Falls. Gives everyone the wrong impression of our town."

"I'm sure you are right, ma'am," Ben said and he took off his Stetson to show his respect. Tom and Jack followed, somewhat reluctantly. Tom was anxious to get on with this.

"Like I said before, Marshal, if there is anything I can do for you."

"As a matter of fact there is, ma'am. I wonder if Mr. Gadsen is around?"

The woman looked shocked as though a lightning bolt had surged through her. "Oh, God rest his soul, Mr. Gadsen has been dead for three years now. I don't know what to tell you, Marshal."

Tom was surprised and so was Jack. However this setback didn't faze Ben Yoder, who had sized up the situation almost immediately.

"We're looking for young Mr. Gadsen. George Gadsen," Ben said.

"Of course," the woman said and she was suitably flustered. "You'll find him and his new bride at the Gadsen house. It's just west of town. You can't miss it. The house is two-storied and it's red. The only house for miles. No way you could miss seeing it."

Ben put his hat back on and respectfully tipped it to the woman. "Much obliged. I think we'll be able to find it."

The woman assured him that the three of them would have no trouble whatsoever. But if they did they were to come back to her at once and she would make certain they didn't have to make a second trip for nothing.

"Got all that, Ben?" Tom asked when they were outside and walking down the boardwalk toward the saloon where their horses were tethered.

"If I didn't I'm not coming back for more directions," Ben said.

"You notice that the lady said Mr. Gadsen and his bride were at their house," Jack put in as he managed to sidestep a barrel that was in front of a street-fronted store.

"I did," Ben said.

"So are you thinking the same thing I am?" Tom said.

"And that is?"

"That this Gadsen feller couldn't have been the shooter at Devil's Whip."

Ben walked a few paces forward before replying.

"Seems that way. Still have to go see him. I want some questions answered."

By this time they were in front of the saloon. All three of them untied their horses and slipped easily into their saddles. They turned their horses in the direction the woman at the mercantile had told them and rode out of town. They were in no hurry since none of the three by this time really still believed they had found their man.

As they turned the corner of the main street they headed their horses due west. The land was grassy and hilly. There was a chill wind from the north that whispered in the grass and made the three men turn the collars up on their jackets. Even the overhead sun could not muster enough energy to give the day any warmth. Winter was on its way and Tom hoped that all of this would be taken care of before the first snow began to fall.

The trail they had taken led over the top of a hill. From here they could see the Gadsen house in the distance. A two-storied, red brick house that was sending a tendril of smoke up from one of the houses's chimneys.

"It has to be the place," Tom said.

"Just like the lady said. Only one around for miles," Ben said.

"What desolate country," were Jack's words and he shivered slightly, more from the view than from the climate.

The trail they rode slowly became a road that led up to the front door of the Gadsen place. As they neared the house Tom saw the flicker of a curtain being lifted aside and then hastily dropped back in place. At least there was somebody home and this wouldn't turn out to be a wasted ride.

They dismounted and walked up to the door. Ben took the lead and pounded on the door. All three of them stepped back, not knowing what to expect from the other side of the door.

When it finally opened there stood a woman, buxom and with disheveled hair as though she had only gotten up. She was not pretty but there was an appealing quality about her that made the three men remove their Stetsons almost in unison.

"Yes?" she said and her voice was husky and mellow as a dollop of good wine. She had something that fascinated most men.

Ben swallowed hard and then said, "Ma'am, we're looking for George Gadsen. Is this here where he lives?"

The woman focused her eyes on Ben as if she were seeing him for the very first time. She smiled and that smile made her seem like she was all of fifteen years old.

"This is his house. I'm his wife, Drusilla. What do you want to see my husband about?"

"We're from Valiant. I'm Marshal Ben Yoder and these here are my deputies Tom Cardy and Jack Madrid."

Tom and Jack nodded. Tom was not all that interested in whom George Gadsen had married but Jack was all smiles a mile wide. "Pleased to meet you, Mrs. Gadsen," Jack said and the pleasure was very evident in his voice.

"You wanted to see my husband, Marshal? What about?" the woman repeated.

At that moment Drusilla's name was called and she turned from the door. "Who is it?" came a man's voice. Drusilla looked back at Ben and then towards the interior of the house. "It's a marshal, honey. Wants to talk to you. You been up to something you haven't told me about?"

"Marshal? I'll be right there," the man said and in a few moments the door was opened even further and there stood George Madsen, just as Slim Taylor had described him.

"You want to see me, Marshal?"

"If you are George Gadsen I do," Ben said, sizing up the man.

"That's me. Why don't you and your men

come on inside. Dru, honey, why don't you get the men some coffee or something to drink."

Drusilla smiled at him and then the men and said, "What's your pleasure, men?"

By the way she said this Tom could tell that Mrs. George Gadsen was not a stranger to saloons or where high spirits were sold. It didn't take long to figure out that Drusilla Gadsen had at one time been very familiar with the ways of a sporting gal. George gave her a whack on her rump before she hurried off to bring the coffee that they had all decided upon.

Gadsen led them into the living room. After they had sat down, he asked, "Where you from, Marshal?"

"Valiant. Me and the men rode over early this morning."

"A long ride. Why do you want to see me?"

Ben leaned forward, staring intently at George Gadsen. "About five days ago the stagecoach from Denver was ambushed and the driver and shotgun were killed. The stagecoach went over Devil's Whip and all four of the passengers died in the crash."

George nodded. "I heard about it. What's that got to do with me?"

"One of the passengers that was killed was Frank Tyler. Maybe you know of him?"

Gadsen didn't blink an eye or show any sign of remorse on hearing this news.

"Yeah, I know of him. Too bad," was all that George Gadsen had to say.

"Would you mind telling us where you were about five days ago, Mr. Gadsen?" Ben asked as Drusilla came into the room. She was carrying a tray of cups filled with coffee.

"Five days ago?" Drusilla said. "Why, I can tell you where George was. He was with me. That was our wedding day."

Tom looked at Jack and then Ben. If she was telling the truth then there was nothing more to be said or done. If she wasn't, it was just their word against hers and George Gadsen.

"You folks married here in Bad Falls?" Tom asked. "Of course you have witnesses if you did."

"We were married in Laramie," George said coolly. "That's where I met my Drusilla. She just dropped into my life like rain on a dry, dry desert."

Drusilla blew George a kiss and then handed the men their coffee. Tom took a sip but it was too hot and too sweet to drink. Probably Drusilla had this in mind and knew that the men wouldn't linger over their coffee if it tasted this foul.

"You got some proof of that?" Ben asked, trying hard not to make a face after taking a big gulp of coffee.

"Our license," George replied smugly. "Would you get it for the gentleman, honey." It was more of a statement than a command. He acted as though he were getting bored with their company. Tom rarely took an instant dislike to anybody, but in the case of George Gadsen he was willing to make an exception.

Drusilla brought the license to George who indicated with his head to take it to Ben. Ben merely glanced at it while Drusilla still held it in her hands. There was no way he could refute what he saw. George Gadsen wasn't their man, although he would have given anything if he had been.

"Sorry we took up so much of your time, Mr. Gadsen," Ben said and got to his feet.

"Do you really think I would try to kill Frank Taylor in front of so many witnesses? Then you and the folks in Valiant are a whole lot dumber than a bunch of wall-eyed jackasses."

Tom couldn't resist. "I'm sure you would know a wall-eyed jackass Mr. Gadsen, since it's plain that you've had a lot of truck in that business."

"Get the hell out of my house," Gadsen said. "And if you ever show your faces around my place again I might try some target practice, just for fun."

"If you did try that on me," Jack said, meeting

Gadsen's smirking gaze with his steely blue eyes, "you'd better make it a good one, 'cause it would be your last."

As they left by the front door Gadsen slammed it shut behind them with such force that a window shattered in the stained-glass door.

Riding away, Tom couldn't resist one last look at the Gadsen house. As he did so he saw Drusilla standing at the window watching them. There was something like fear in her eyes and she held herself rigid like she was frightened of something. The curtains were parted and started to fall but not before Tom saw a hand roughly grab Drusilla and yank her away from his view. Tom could imagine what had happened to Drusilla after that.

"He may not be the hombre that done the shootin' at Devil's Whip but I kind of was hoping he just might have been," Madrid said laconically.

"A little short on good manners, I'd say," said Ben.

"No wonder the Taylor boys had it in for him. Not only is he a buffalo pie and loco but I don't like the way he treats his woman," Tom said.

"With his attitude I don't think he's going to last much longer in Bad Falls," Ben said prophetically.

"Looks like we're back where we started," Tom said.

"Not really." Ben looked over at Tom who rode to his right. "We don't have one suspect anymore."

"Guess you're right. So what now?" Tom said.

"Does this mean we're un-deputized?" Jack said and took out his plug of tobacco from his jacket pocket.

"Let me sleep on that. For now you two are still my deputies."

Jack took a bite from the plug and said, "No chance, I suppose, Tom and me drawin' any pay for all this?"

"You're right, no chance. For now."

"Figured."

On the long ride back to Valiant Tom thought about what his plans would be. Now that Gadsen had turned out not to be the shooter he would have to concentrate on the next likely suspect. That could only mean Rune Ballard. Tom wondered if he was still gone from Valiant. When they got back he and Jack would make another run to Ballard's shack. If Ballard turned out not to be the guilty one then Tom had no idea who might have committed the murders.

The wind had picked up once they reached the foothills. Heavy, dark clouds swirled about the sky, hiding the sun. Images of Caroline suddenly came back to taunt Tom. Caroline on their wedding day, radiantly beautiful and happy. Caroline at the supper table after Tom had washed up and was filled with a good, work-tired feeling. Caroline by lamplight, sitting on the floor, leaning against him while she read from some book that she treasured. Scenes spun across his mind. These were painful, choking memories that rekindled Tom's fires of revenge.

Shortly after noon they rested under the protection of some poplars as they ate the jerky and drank fresh, cool water from a clean, meandering stream nearby.

While Ben nodded and finally fell into a deep sleep punctuated by sudden bursts of snoring, Jack and Tom talked.

"You been thinking about Rune Ballard same as me, haven't you, Tom?"

Tom stuck a dry blade of grass into his mouth and cocked an eyebrow. "He just might be our man. Just wondering why he left town so soon after the stagecoach was wrecked. Word travels fast in Valiant. He must have had something on his conscience and he figured he'd better make himself scarce for a while."

"My thoughts exactly. This wild goose chase just makes me feel it's Ballard we should be after. All this riding was just so much prairie smoke."

"Think we ought to ride over to his place once

we get back to Valiant? He might be back from wherever he was off to."

"I was planning on doing just that. If Rune isn't our man then we'll just keep on searching."

Jack snapped a twig he had been holding in his hands. "Ever think it might just be some ornery polecat who had a grudge against the stage line? He might have set out to do what he wanted and then high-tailed it clean out of the county."

"That crossed my mind," Tom said. "Only my gut tells me that this gunslinger is still in Valiant."

"You got more at stake then I have. Whatever you think. I'm with you all the way."

Tom looked at the windburned face of Jack Madrid. He was glad Jack was on his side. Madrid could be a mighty powerful friend and an equally powerful and deadly enemy.

"You're a good friend, Jack."

"Just part of the job, now that I'm a deputy," Madrid answered and there was an ironic twist to his mouth.

Ben stirred and woke up with a snort. He rubbed his eyes and sat up.

"Sorry, must have dozed off. You ready to saddle up again?"

"Any time you say, Ben." Tom was already on his feet and going to tend his mustang.

"Let's ride," Ben said and Madrid tossed aside

the twig he had been worrying in his rough, cal-
loused hands.

When they were about a mile from Valiant Ben
said, "Ever think of selling that land of yours,
Tom? Ever have any thoughts along those lines?"

Without a moment's hesitation Tom said,
"Nope."

"Seems to me we've been though this kind of
jawin' before," Ben said.

"We have."

They didn't say anything for the rest of the
way to Valiant. But as they neared the town a
lone rider came at a fast trot toward them. When
he was near enough for them to see that it was
Toby Hanks, the town farrier, the man waved a
quick arm to them.

Riding up close to them, Toby drew in on the
reins.

"What's the big rush, Toby?" Ben asked.

"We need you in town, Marshal," Toby burst
out. Toby, a huge, hairy hulk of a man with a
lantern jaw and strong, powerful hands, normally
wasn't a man given to excitement. Today, however, he was sucking in air and breathing hard
like a bear with a burr.

"Trouble?" Tom asked.

"Bunch of drunken waddies been shootin' up
the town and ridin' hell for leather down the
streets."

"Kinda early in the day for that, ain't it?" Jack said.

"Tell that to them drovers," Toby said. "You goin' to do anything, Marshal?"

Ben turned to face Tom and then Jack. "Let's go, Deputies. Got to earn our pay."

"What pay?" Jack said. But he dug his spurs into his pinto's flanks and headed for Valiant alongside Tom and Ben.

Chapter Seven

In the Bank of Valiant, in the office of the manager Jubal Johnson, all was quiet. For a while there Jubal had been worried. The shots fired, the noisy, drunken shouts of the cowboys and the thunderous sound of their horses had given him cause for alarm. Where was Marshal Yoder when he was needed? Somebody had told Jubal he was out of town for the day.

"If I would just walk away for a day what would people do?" Jubal had said to Elva Kleindorf.

"That's different, Mr. Johnson," Elva replied. "Ben is the law. You are only a banker."

Jubal had gone back to his office a little miffed at Elva. He had never liked the woman and would be glad when he never had to come into the bank and face her every day. That wouldn't be too far in the future if he had his way. Elva was good at her job. Actually there were two things she was good at. Her job and bringing him news from the outside world.

Jubal sat in the comfort of his office. It was sparse and unadorned, only the necessary accoutrements that he used in its daily operations. The only concession he made to any fripperies was the gilted mirror that hung on the wall.

This ascetic simplicity didn't extend to his private residence, which was just outside of Valiant. It was richly decorated and had a wall lined with rare books of first edition. This love for pleasurable amenities and good living was given him by his mother back East where Jubal was born and reared. He grudgingly gave her credit for instilling this in him but that was all he gave her.

Jubal's affections were not for people, kin, or close friends. When his father and brothers had fought in the War he had chosen to come westward and felt not remorse when they were all three killed at Lookout Mountain. "What fools they were. I cannot see giving my life up for strangers. Or for a cause."

Hearing from another communiqué that his mother and sister had both perished from an outbreak of diphtheria didn't move him to tears or sympathy. Jubal was far too busy learning the banking trade. He rose quickly in Valiant from clerk to manager. Jubal was excellent when it came to ciphering and this held him in good stead.

"Someday," he said aloud to the mirror, "I'll leave Valiant. This is only a minor detour in my life."

Then Jubal sat back and indulged himself in one of his few luxuries. A fat, hand-rolled cigar.

Ben Yoder, Tom, and Jack quickly rode the short distance to Valiant. At the turnoff to his stables Toby left them. He first apologized for his attitude.

"Just let them waddies get the better of me," Toby said.

"Forget it," Ben assured him. "We'll take care of them."

After Toby had gone Ben said, "You two ready for a little action?"

"Okay by me," Jack said, running one hand over the butt of his six-gun.

"We're with you, Ben," Tom said, who had silently been in agreement with Madrid.

They tethered their horses not too far from the saloon. Even from this distance they could hear the yahooing and commotion going on in The Busted Nugget.

"Sounds like they're having a whoopin' time in there," was Jack's assessment.

"A little too much," Ben said.

"Can we arrest them when they're just inside having a few drinks?" Tom asked.

"Got a complaint from a citizen," Ben said. "We can arrest them for disturbing the peace."

At that moment a six-gun erupted and a bullet thudded into the dirt-encrusted street, sending up a quick puff of dust.

"That's all we need," Ben said. "You men ready?"

"We're with you," Tom answered.

They eased their way down the boardwalk until they were in front of the saloon. Ben motioned for Tom to follow him and for Madrid to take the other side of the batwinged doors.

Inside they could hear the sound of more gunshots and a yell from one of the drovers. Raising one hand, Ben used the other to pull out his Colt. Tom and Jack followed suit. When Ben lowered his upraised hand they burst through the batwinged doors.

The saloon was blue with cigarette and gun smoke. Several men were in the corner crouched behind chairs and tables to hide themselves from the gunslingers who were on the other side of the room. Covering Big Bert at the bar was a drunken, dirt-coated drover who lifted a glass of whiskey to his lips when he saw Ben and Tom and Jack.

"Drop it," Ben said to the man with the gun on Big Bert.

The man thought for a second but it was the wrong decision and he trained the gun on Ben who squeezed off two bullets that hit the man in the shoulder with such force that he spun around, blood spurting out from the wound.

Big Bert ducked behind the bar just as the other drovers realized what had happened. The four waddies' guns began to blaze and Tom and Jack and Ben returned their fire.

"Behind that table, quick!" Tom shouted and he made a dive as Ben did the same. Jack's heavy body fell against Tom and he cried out, "I been hit. My arm!"

Tom tried to tend the fallen Madrid but Jack said, "Don't bother with me; I'll be all right. Just watch out for those drovers."

Seeing Jack with blood oozing out from his right arm brought out blind rage in Tom. He jacked some more shells into his six-shooter and fanned the trigger as bullets found their mark and two of the drovers dropped to the floor. The other two tried to make it to the door but Big Bert had pulled out his Winchester and had it aimed at the heart of one of them and Ben fired his weapon, sending the six-shooter spinning out of the other drover's hand.

The two waddies held up their hands and surrendered. The effects of the rot-gut had worn off very fast. They kept saying over and over, "Don't shoot! Don't shoot!"

"How is Jack?" Ben asked, not taking his eyes off the two men.

"He's losing some blood. Somebody get the doc!" Tom said. One of the patrons who had been covering behind a table in the far corner ran for help. Tom took off her kerchief and used it to try and slow the flow of blood.

"Big Bert," Ben called out. "Keep your eyes on those two men by the door. I'm going to see what damage we did to the others."

Ben walked across the room while Big Bert came out from behind the bar, his Winchester leveled with deadly intent. The two drovers kept their hands in the air and pleaded with the barkeep not to shoot.

"I ought to make daylight through you two. Look what you and those other polecats did to my place. You'll pay for this. You'll pay for every last splinter I have to put back."

The two men assured Big Bert that they would gladly pay for all the damages, that they just had too much to drink, that they would never, ever touch rot-gut liquor to their lips again. Maybe

they went a little too far in their apology but Big
Bert accepted their promise.

Ben found that there were no dead among the
human debris. The man who had held the gun
drunkenly on Big Bert and had then mistakenly
turned it on him was the worst of the lot. The
three men lay moaning and groaning, clutching
their wounds.

Doc Kreugger came in hurriedly. He looked
around trying to decide who needed the quickest
attention. "Another barroom brawl. As long as
The Busted Nugget is in business I won't lack for
patients."

He decided, since he was on the side of law
and order, to fix Jack Madrid up first. The bullet
had made a clean exit and hadn't touched a bone
in Jack's arm. Dr. Kreugger put some painful as-
tringent on the wound that made even stoic Jack
Madrid flinch. Then he bandaged the wound.

"You rest that arm for a few days, you hear,"
Doc said in his gruff, gravel-voiced way. Then
he headed across the room to minister to the other
wounded. On the way he stopped at the bar and
tilted the contents of a bottle into a shot glass
which he downed in a quick gulp.

"Just for fortification," he said as he wiped his
lips with his sleeve and then went about his work.

"You're going to the ranch," Tom said to Jack.
"Like the doc said, you need to rest a few days."

"I'll be all right," Jack said, trying to use his right arm, but he grimaced and, at last, consented to listen to Tom's advice.

When Doc Kreugger had finished his work, he closed his black valise and poured himself another drink. "You putting these men in jail, Marshal?"

"Right away," was Ben's firm answer.

"Good, so I'll know where they are. I'll need to see them later to change those dressings."

With that, Doc Kreugger downed his whiskey and walked wearily and somewhat unsteadily out of The Busted Nugget.

"Come on Tom, help me herd these drovers over to the jail."

Tom nodded. "You wait here, Jack. I'll be back as soon as I can."

"Forget that," Jack said. "I can still walk. I'm coming along to the jail."

"Suit yourself," Tom said and gave Jack's good arm a gentle, good-natured punch. "Let's go."

Big Bert was still aiming his Winchester at the two men. "I'm going too," he said. "I'll stick with these two like molasses on flapjacks."

The batwing doors opened as Big Bert urged the two men out. Tom and Ben rounded up the other three and, at gunpoint, motioned for them to follow Big Bert.

On the way out of the saloon Tom motioned to Jack to follow. None of them was prepared for what they found outside the Nugget. Almost all the townsfolk were gathered around, gawking at the drovers as they came out bandaged and blood-smeared.

Tom only recalled seeing the face of Elva Kleindorf looking on with disapproval and clicking her teeth. They were all temporarily stalled in their march to the jailhouse.

"Serves 'em right!"

"Throw them in and toss the key away!"

"They should be tarred and feathered!"

"Run 'em out of town tied to the rear end of a jackass!"

These were some of the comments erupting from the crowd.

Since they temporarily couldn't move, Jack turned to Tom and said, "What about Rune Ballard? What are we going to do about him?"

"*We* aren't going to do anything. I'm putting you to bed at the ranch and then I'm going to Ballard's shack. I'm going to find out what he knows about Caroline's death if I have to blast it out of him."

"If it wasn't for this arm you know I'd be right there with you, Tom."

Tom touched Jack on his good shoulder. "I know. You've already been a big help."

By this time Ben had poked a hole in the throng and he motioned for Tom and Jack to follow him. Most of the crowd followed them down the boardwalk to the jailhouse. Along the way there were taunts and jeering. Tom was beginning to have an uncomfortable feeling and was glad when they finally got to the jail.

"Now hear me," Ben said, still holding his six-shooter in his gun hand. "I'm putting these here men in jail. If any of you want to join them just stick around and keep making noise."

There were a few grumblings among the townsfolk but gradually the crowd dispersed and drifted away.

Ben waved his gun at the three men. "Inside." They hurried inside thankful that the crowd hadn't been in the mood for a necktie party.

After Ben and his prisoners came Big Bert and the two drovers followed by Tom and Jack. Once inside Ben unlocked the iron doors to the cells and motioned for the prisoners to step inside.

"How long we gotta stay here, Marshal?" one of the uninjured men asked.

"Depends on what the owner of the saloon has to say about it."

Big Bert finally lowered his Winchester to his side.

"I'll sleep on it tonight. I'll be in my nice comfortable bed while you drovers try to rest on them bunks."

"Honest, sir," said one of the now stone-sober men, "we'll pay you for everything. If we have to ride herd the rest of our lives to do it."

"You just might have to do that, by the looks of my saloon," said Big Bert. "Hell, I don't mind a little roughhouse but you got carried away."

"Guess maybe we did."

It was close to an apology so Big Bert walked over to the door and opened it. Before he left he said, "Ben, thanks. That goes for you too, Tom and Jack. Sorry you got winged in the fracas, Madrid. Tell Doc Kreugger I'll pay for the damage."

With that Big Bert walked out of the jailhouse. The drovers settled down for a long night. The wounded lay down on their bunks and tried to fall asleep. The others just sat on the floor and waited for the night to be over and done with.

"How's the arm, Jack?" Ben asked in a soft, concerned voice.

"Stings a little. Got any coffee left?"

"Sure. You just sit a spell. I'll rustle you up a cup."

Jack sat down and Tom drew up a chair but he didn't sit. Instead he followed Ben over to where the coffee was kept. He found himself a mug and poured it to the brim with the thick, hot liquid. Then he followed Ben back to where Madrid was sitting. Ben handed the wounded comrade the cup. "It's hot," he said.

"Won't feel it unless it's hot as fresh-blown lava," Jack said, taking the cup and gulping down a big swig of the coffee. It was hot and it brought tears to his eyes.

"Been quite a day," Ben said.

"I'll agree with you on that score," Tom said. "Too bad we didn't find our man over at Bad Falls. That Gadsen would have made a great prisoner."

"Nice lookin' wife," Jack put in. "Didn't get treated right by him though."

"Wonder where the Taylor boys were? Guess maybe they were taking care of their brother," Tom said and took a swift swallow from his cup.

"Don't think we've heard the last of that Gadsen. I can see how that Taylor boy might have taken his gal away from him. Anyone would be better than him," Ben said, straddling a chair.

"At least we all agree on something," Tom said, and he looked at Ben who was frowning. Then Ben laughed as Tom joined in with him.

They both laughed hard and long. Madrid looked at them as though they had gone loco. Then he saw that for Tom it was just a release from all the stress he had been under the past few days. Ben enjoyed sharing in the release he got that went along with his long, childhood friend-ship.

Their laughter was cut short when the door opened and Jubal Johnson stood in the doorway. He was a tall, gaunt man who looked years older than his thirty-two. He hesitated as the three men turned to look at him.

"Yes, Jubal," Ben said. "What can I do for you?"

Jubal looked around and saw that Ben was not alone.

"I was just wondering, Marshal, wondering about those men who were shooting up the town. You know the bank has a lot of its depositors' money and we wouldn't want anything to happen to it, would we."

Ben leaned back and slowly raised his cup to his mouth and took a casual sip of the strained mud.

"No need to worry, Jubal. With the help of my deputies that little problem is all taken care of."

"Evening, Tom," Jubal said and there was a whisper of a smile on his wiry lips. "Well, I'm certainly pleased to learn that, Marshal Yoder. We can't be too careful now can we."

"They're locked up all nice and cozy," Ben said. "We'll see tomorrow if charges will be made."

"I guess that answers my question," Jubal said. "I won't bother you any further."

"No bother, Jubal," Ben said. "I'm here whenever you need me."

Jubal held his tongue. He was thinking about the marshal leaving town that morning. If he had been here there wouldn't be a need for these louts to be locked up. He should have been here to quell any disturbances before they began. Instead he said, "I'll remember that, Marshal. Guess I'll be running along. Still have some work at the bank that needs to be done."

"You work too hard," Tom said. "Haven't ever heard of you takin' a vacation. Don't you ever do anything but count money?"

Jubal managed a weak smile. "I have my pleasures, Tom. But since I enjoy what I'm doing I can't see taking time off to just sit around doing nothing but think about my work."

"Like Tom said, you work too hard, Jubal," Ben said. "Haven't you ever thought about going someplace, someplace like San Francisco or Denver or even Cheyenne?"

"Valiant is my home. This is where I have my house. Maybe someday I'll take a trip. Maybe sometime in the near future."

"You should think about it," Tom said.

Jubal looked at Tom and then Ben and then slowly nodded his head. "I'll do that."

He didn't say another word but just turned and went into the night.

"He's a hard worker," Jack said. "But I think he's too much of a loner."

"That's his business," Tom said. Then he got to his feet. "Let's get back to the ranch, Jack. I think we could use a little shut-eye."

"No argument here," Jack said as he eased himself out of the chair. "Much obliged for the coffee, Marshal. Had the kick of a Brahma bull."

"You take care of that arm," Ben said. "I'll ask Doc Kreugger to swing by the ranch tomorrow and check on you."

"No need for that," Jack protested.

"Feel better if I did," was Ben's reply. "And thanks to both of you for riding shotgun today."

"We're deputies, remember," Tom said. "Just part of the duty."

"Get out of here," Ben said with a chuckle. "Before I let you join those other hombres inside."

Tom and Jack left the jailhouse and ambled down the boardwalk to where they had tethered their horses. It was a chilly night and the moon was icy gray in the star-speckled sky.

"How you holding up?" Tom said as they both slipped their feet into their stirrups and were into their saddles in a blink.

"Getting a little woozy," Madrid answered.

"Must be from all that blood you lost at the saloon. Think you can make it to the ranch all right? It's still a little ride."

"Sure thing," Jack said.

Even at that Tom kept a wary eye on his compatriot as they rode out of town and toward the ranch.

Tom found that he was beginning to get a little weary himself after all the riding and the fracas at The Busted Nugget. One thing he came to see was that the pain in his gut from losing Caroline wasn't as bad as it had been. His mind had been taken off her what with the trip to Bad Falls and George Gadsen and then the shootout at the saloon. Still, now that it was quiet and he listened to the wind moaning through the brush alongside the trail, he renewed his pledge to himself that he would find and punish whoever had killed his wife.

When they got to the ranch Tom helped Jack Madrid into the house. Madrid was unsteady on his feet and had to lean on Tom from the hitchrail to the house.

"You're staking out my bed," Tom said. "No argument."

"Thanks," Jack said, too dogtired and weak to offer up any argument.

After Jack had gone to bed, asleep as soon as

his head hit the pillow, Tom stretched out on the floor with a couple of blankets to cover him.

His last thoughts were of Caroline, and, more unpleasantly, Rune Ballard.

Chapter Eight

It was late, too late for Rune to saddle up and ride into Valiant. He was thirsty, dry-bone thirsty. He lifted the bottle of whiskey he had been gulping all evening and tilted it above his lips. One amber drop seeped from the mouth of the bottle onto his parched, cracked lips.

"Nothing but my bad eye in there winking back at me," he said and hurled the bottle across the filthy, unkempt room and heard it smash against the wall. If he walked around during the night barefoot he would sure as tootin' cut his feet. But none of that mattered to Ballard right now. Right now he needed another drink. Real bad.

He had reached that point in his drinking when

he was almost ready to fall onto his vermin-infested, sweat-stained bed and fall asleep.

Rune needed to sleep. At least then he didn't have to think about his life. This wasn't the way it was supposed to turn out. It wasn't the way he had planned it. There was supposed to be money, lots of money. Instead all he had gotten were a few coins with the promise of more.

"Promises! Promises! That's all I ever get. Well, dammit, let me tell you. By damn no more promises. No more promises or else."

Rune's voice rose to a loud pitch. But out here who would hear him? This was his shack and he had a right. Everybody had always tried to shut Rune Ballard up, all his life. Or they tried to hurt him. He remembered his old man back in Missouri who used to beat him with a knobby oak limb regularly. Rune couldn't ever do anything to please him. Not like his older brother Orville. Orry was the apple of his pappy's eye. The sun rose and set on good old Orry. But his pap had hit Rune one time too many when he was too big to take that kind of beating anymore.

"Got him, didn't I. Got him nice and good." Rune's voice echoed around the shack and out into the dark, still night.

Rune had picked up a shovel and made mush out of his pap's head. Then he had saddled up the old, wind-scarred mare and lit out. Rune never once looked back. But he had learned something back there. He had learned he had a profession. A profession in killing. He thought he might feel something after he had done in his pap but he didn't. He didn't feel a thing.

After that, killing became a way of life for Rune. If he wanted something someone had, he would just wait till nobody was looking and either take it or kill the owner.

So far Ballard had been lucky. He hadn't been caught. But he was smart enough to know that he was pushing his luck.

Here in Valiant he had found a place where he could be away from people. They were the reason he was the way he was. Every time he got around people, something bad always happened. So, here he was a mile from town and all by himself. Just the way he liked it.

"You promised me more money!" Rune yelled out. He kicked at a rickety chair he had found at the dump and missed. Rune tried to regain his balance but he toppled over on the floor. He cussed again and struggled to get to his feet.

"If you don't pay me I'm going to pass the word around. You bet I will. I'm going to tell them who it was paid me to shoot them two guys on the stagecoach and spook the horses."

His voice was roaring loud now. A stranger passing by out there might easily have made out what he was saying. But Rune didn't care. He'd done his part; he'd done his job. Now, by the devil's rump, he would be paid for that.

"I need a drink! I need a good long swig," he yelled out in his drunken, slurring voice.

He was staggering around the shack bumping into chairs and boxes and old oily rags when someone stepped into the doorway. Sensing the presence of another person, Rune slowly turned, trying to focus his red-rimmed eyes. When he did his lips curled in a mocking grin.

"So it's you. 'Bout time you showed up. Got something for me?"

The man nodded and reached inside his jacket. "Yes. I've got something for you."

Rune only had a split second to think as the bullet from the small derringer sunk with deadly force into the center of his forehead. He sank to the floor and a thin line of blood trickled from the wound.

The man pocketed the gun and, as silently as he had entered, went out into the cold, dark night.

"You hungry yet, Jack?" Tom called out from the kitchen where he was cracking eggs into a cast-iron skillet. The aroma of fresh brewed coffee and sizzling bacon hung in the air.

"Could eat a gallopin' horse," came the answer from the bedroom.

Tom put some plates and silverware on the table and poured coffee into two mugs. It wasn't as good as Caroline's but then nobody could hold a flickerin' candle to his late wife in the cooking department.

When Jack came into the kitchen he still looked gray and weak. Tom knew that it would take food and rest to get Jack well again.

"Smells mighty tempting," Jack said as he slowly dropped into a chair at the table.

Tom put the platter of eggs and bacon and biscuits in the center of the table and said, "Dig in, Jack. Sorry I didn't fry any taters but I'm just not too good with them."

"You won't find me complaining," Madrid said as he used his good hand to scoop out some eggs. He tried to spear some bacon but to no avail.

"Use your fingers, Jack. That's what I'm doing," said Tom, solving the problem.

As they ate Jack asked Tom, "You going over to Ballard's place today?"

Tom took a swig from his mug of coffee and said, "After I check with the boys out on the range. Should show them that I'm still interested in raising cattle."

"They'll do a good job from what I know of the Dusault family. Want me to ride along with you?"

Tom put a stop to that kind of thinking with a

quick shake of his head. His clear blue eyes stared unblinkingly at Madrid.

"You are stayin' here and resting."

"By whose orders?"

"Me and Doc Kreugger. I can't use a one-handed gunslinger. I want you to get well so you can help me run this spread."

Jack scooped another egg onto his plate. "I ain't sick. Just got a winged arm."

"Well, that winged arm is going to stay in that sling until Doc Kreugger says to take it off."

Jack squinted an eye at Tom.

"Wouldn't bet any good money on that. When I'm ready to ride again no saw-bones is going to stop me. And that goes for you too, Tom Cardy."

Tom didn't take offense. He knew Jack and a lot of what he was saying was just plain bluff. But a lot was plain true and Jack would in the end be the person who would decide his destiny.

"Good enough," Tom said. A half-hour later he was in the saddle and headed for the range where the Dusault boys were working the herd.

Tom couldn't help a faint chuckle as he thought about Jack and his stubbornness. He was so much like Tom in that respect he could have easily passed for his older brother. Then that chuckle quickly faded as Tom thought once again about Caroline. What right did he have to any fun or laughter when the murderer of his wife still was alive and enjoying life?

Tom's jaw set in a hard line as he urged his horse into a fast trot so that he could reach the Dusaults and see how things were going.

The two Dusaults were patiently watching the herd of cattle grazing. Louis, the older of the two, was singing a song he had heard his papa sing over and over while he split kindling for the fireplace.

> "Ottalie, Oh, Ottalie.
> It was a dark and dismal day,
> The day you went away,
> Sing, sing, away, away.
> Away, sing, Ottalie."

Conrade, the younger brother, who was always cheerful and rarely lost his temper, leaned on his saddle horn. "Looks like we got company, Lou. I see a rider coming."

It didn't take them long to figure out that the lone rider was their boss, Tom Cardy. The two Dusaults were easygoing but hard-working men. This they had learned from their father. They were always eager to help Tom out because they knew that someday they would marry and have a house and cattle of their own. They were grateful to him for letting them get all the experience they could.

Tom hailed them as he approached. He could always rely on Louis and Conrade to be dependable. He paid well and they did a good day's work.

"Morning, men," Tom Cardy said as he approached and reined in his horse. This, calling them men, the boys also liked. Tom treated them like he would any seasoned drover.

"Any problems?"

"We found a hole in the fence on the north side of the range. Not big enough for a calf to skinny through but we fixed it."

"Many thanks. I was worried about that part of the fence when I put it up. You two don't know how you ease my mind."

Conrade's face beamed with the compliment. Louis quietly accepted the praise.

"How's it going with you, Mr. Cardy?" Conrade asked. He was referring to Caroline and Tom's period of grief.

"Still looking, Conrade," Tom answered. "But I'll find the man yet."

"Heard there was a little shoot-out at The Busted Nugget yesterday," Louis said. "You know anything about that?"

"I was there."

Louis and Conrade both seemed to be interested. "Are you all right?" Conrade asked.

"Fine. But Madrid took one in the arm. He's at the ranch resting up. Just a bunch of liquored-up drovers. They spent the night in jail but I don't think Big Bert will ask to have them held. As long as they pay for the damages, that's all he's interested in."

"We miss out on everything," Conrade said, sounding somewhat disappointed.

"Don't be too sure of that," Tom said. "Wasn't all that exciting. In a shootout you just pray the next bullet doesn't have you in mind. You men are better off out here on the range."

"Guess so," Louis said. Then he looked at his brother and Tom and decided that Tom was right. He wasn't always looking for adventure like his younger brother. Conrade was still too young to know that you can get really hurt playing around with six-shooters.

Tom talked to the two boys, or men as he called them though they were still in their early years, for about a half-hour. It was lonesome out on the range and he knew the feeling of hungering for any news about what was going on in Valiant or anywhere.

"Pardon me, Mr. Cardy," Conrade said. "Don't aim to pry. Maybe it's none of my business but has the Marshal found out anything about Mrs. Cardy's death?"

"Connie!" Louis said. "What's the matter with you? Didn't I tell you not to ask questions like that?"

"It's all right, Louis, I'm doin' better," Tom said. "Me and Marshal Yoder and Madrid went over to Bad Falls yesterday. Had a lead on somebody. Didn't come to nothing. That hombre had himself a good accountin' for where he was when it happened. But we'll find who done it. Don't worry none about that."

Telling the Dusaults to keep up the good work, Tom rode away, headed for Valiant.

There was no reason to stop by the ranch house to check on Madrid; he would be all right. Now was the time to ride over to Ballard's shack. Maybe by this time he would have come back. Maybe Ballard hadn't gone very far and he and Madrid had just dropped by at the wrong time.

In his heart Tom felt that Ballard was the shooter. Yet, somewhere in the dark, murky depths of his mind, he had a strange feeling that if Ballard was done away with, it wasn't over. He didn't know why he felt this way, just a hunch.

Tom touched the holster to check on his Colt. He felt the smooth, thick texture of the butt-handle and pulled it out to be sure there were bullets in all the chambers. Satisfied, he spun it around on his forefinger in show-off mood before sinking it once more into the holster.

In the distance stood the mountains and foothills bathed in chilly autumn purples and grays. Patches of glistening early snow sparkled in what sunlight touched them. Overhead a large flock of honking geese winged their way across the sky in an expert V formation.

Nearing Valiant, Tom saw to his right a cloud of dust stirred up by about five horsemen heading with dogged determination toward town. As they drew near Tom could see they were strangers, but from their hunched shoulders and the ornery looks on their faces they were angry about something.

Tom decided to follow them into Valiant. It looked to him that they were up to no good. Maybe Ben would need some help. If he did Tom would be right there, since he was now deputized to do so.

The column of men funneled out to two abreast as they reined their horses to a slow trot. They slowly proceeded down the main street of town. As they passed the farrier shop, Toby Hanks came out to watch them. Tom brought his mustang to a stop before the farrier and said, "I don't like the looks of those drovers."

"I'm with you," Toby said. "If you ask me they

look like a trail boss and his men. Only one reason they're in town."

"To get his men out of jail," Tom completed the thought. "I think Ben will need some help."

"Hold on a second, I'll get my six-shooter and be right with you. Time we back our marshal and stand behind him."

There were a couple of men lounging inside the farrier's business and when they heard from Toby what was happening they grabbed their rifles and joined up.

"Looks a little more even this way," Tom said as the four of them walked down the street not too far behind the newcomers. Other townsfolk saw what was happening and some of them called out to wait until they got their guns. Others moved quickly away, not wanting to be involved in the confrontation.

From the store windows Tom saw people gawking and some of the women shaking their heads in disapproval. Tom was proud of the men who had chosen up sides and were walking with them. As they passed the bank Tom caught a glimpse of Jubal Johnson, who was watching the proceedings with keen interest. It didn't surprise Tom any that the banker wasn't one of them. Jubal was a loner and he also had a bank to run. Jubal was far from being a novice when it came to gun handling because Tom had once seen him bottle practicing with his Stevens 25-20 and he was nobody's simpleton when it came to picking the bottles off the corral fenceposts.

Tom forgot all about Jubal as they neared the jailhouse. Word must have traveled ahead of the men because Ben was standing, straddle-legged in front of the jail. His hands were loose at his side but there was a tenseness in him like a rattlesnake ready to strike.

"What are you men doing here?" Ben asked. "I hope you come peacefully."

The trail boss leaned forward on the saddle horn. He spoke in a calm, hoarse voice, almost like a raspy whisper. "I'm missin' some men from my outfit. Hear tell they just might be locked up in your jail."

"Might be," Ben said slowly. "All the men I got behind bars got a reason to be there."

"Don't doubt your word, Marshal," the trail boss said with equal slowness. "Wonder if I could see the men. We don't want no trouble. Only we ain't the runnin' type on the other hand."

Ben stood his ground. "Don't want no trouble either. You can come in and have a look-see. The other men will have to stay where they are."

The other cowboys set up a caterwauling that might have led to some bad trouble had it not been for the arrival of Tom and Toby and the fifteen other townspeople, all armed. "We'll just stay here with you men and keep you company," Tom said.

"Who gave you the right?" one of the drovers said.

"I did," Ben answered before Tom could say anything. "He's my deputy. You'll answer to him while I'm inside."

If that didn't sit well with the men, they didn't speak up. They looked at the gathering of townspeople and decided not to make a stand. After all these were the people who bought their beef, the merchants who sold them provisions, the family men who were raising children who might someday be playing with their children when, and if, they ever married.

Before very long the trail boss and Ben came out the front door. It was apparent that the men locked up inside were part of his outfit.

"So what's going to happen to my men, Marshal?" the trail boss asked.

"That all depends on the owner of the saloon. It's up to him whether I keep the men locked up or not."

Out of the crowd stepped Big Bert. "We can end all this right now," he said. "As far as I'm concerned if the men pay for the damages to my place they can go free. That's all I care about. Just can't see locking a man up for having a little bit too much to drink."

Right there, out in front of the jail, the matter was solved.

"I'll stand good for the men," the trail boss said. "If they can't come up with the money I'll pay the difference. And I'll take it out of their wages."

"Fair enough," Big Bert said.

"Come on inside," Ben said. "I'll free the men."

The mood changed all around. The four horsemen were smiling and speaking to the townspeople who were surrounding them. What was once a potentially dangerous situation had been averted. There was even some good-natured joshing and laughter among the crowd. Tom was relieved. Not only for himself but for Ben who soon appeared again with the incarcerated men. A cheer went up from their fellow drovers.

The outfit assembled together and the trail boss said, "You take us to your place, barkeep, and we'll square things away."

"Follow me," Big Bert said and he was smiling beneath that bushy, caterpillar mustache that hid the ugly scar he had gotten years ago in a brou-haha in a border town in Texas.

Not only did the cowpokes go to The Busted Nugget but most of the townsfolk. All those whose wives hadn't been watching, that is.

When they were gone Ben walked over to

Tom. "Glad you came along when you did. That was gettin' a little hot and heavy for a while."

"Figured something was up when I saw them riding into town. Guess my hunch paid off."

"What you doing in town? Not that I ain't glad to see you."

Tom hoped that Ben wouldn't see through what he was about to say. Even as kids he found it hard to fool his best friend.

"I was out on the range checking on the Dusault men and I decided to come into town to see what was happening here. Nothing more than that."

If he hadn't fooled Ben the marshal of Valiant didn't show it. He was probably just grateful that Tom had shown up when he did.

"Want some coffee?"

Tom shook his head. "Not this morning. I'd better be gettin' along. Maybe next time I'm in town."

Ben nodded. Then as Tom turned to walk away he said, "Remember you're still deputized, Tom. In case you run into something that ain't exactly on the up and up."

"I'll remember that," Tom said and straightened his back as he walked away from the jailhouse.

Chapter Nine

Tom resisted the impulse to turn his head and look back to see if Ben Yoder was still watching him. He knew that he just had to complete the ride to Ballard's shack. He knew he had to at least speak to the man or he would never have any peace.

When he got to Toby's farrier shop the stocky, bushy-haired man was talking to a woman. It wasn't Toby's wife. This was a different, very pretty woman.

"Tom, I want you to meet my cousin, Katherine. She's visiting my wife and me for a few weeks."

Tom touched the brim of his hat out of respect. Katherine smiled at him. Her skin was fair as a wild daisy's and her eyes and hair were a dark brown, almost with a reddish tint to them. When she smiled her eyes sparkled and were vividly alive.

"Pleased to meet you, Tom. Were you with that group of men down at the jail?"

"Ben Yoder, he's the marshal, is a good friend of mine and I wanted to help him out."

Toby folded his thick arms across his wide muscular chest. "Tom's wife passed away a few days ago," he said and the smile faded from Katherine's lips. Instead she looked at him with quiet understanding and then slowly lowered her eyes.

"I'm very sorry, Tom. I didn't catch your last name?"

"It's Cardy. Tom Cardy. I'm getting over it . . . but it's a slow time."

"I know," Katherine said.

"You two have something in common," Toby said in his brash, blundering way. "Katherine lost her husband last year. Scarlet fever, wasn't it?"

Katherine just nodded. Tom waited until she raised her eyes and then he saw in them the suffering that he had missed before.

"Maybe you'll come over for dinner some time while Katherine is here," Toby said. "She doesn't know many folks here in town."

"Now, Toby, Mr. Cardy probably has a lot on

his mind at this time. I don't think he would care to come for supper."

Tom didn't want Katherine to think he had turned into a self-pitying, feel-sorry-for-myself recluse. He spoke up after clearing his throat.

"I'd like that, Toby. Mrs. Dusault is a good cook but a change wouldn't do no harm."

Katherine's smile came back. Tom felt good that he had accepted.

"That's wonderful," Katherine said in a voice that was both mellow-warm and spirited. "Toby will get in touch with you. I plan on being here for a few more weeks."

"Do you like Valiant . . . and I don't know your last name, Katherine."

"Clark. Katherine Clark. And yes, yes, I do like Valiant. It's just the right size and a good place to bring up children."

"You have some kids?"

"No. But someday maybe I'll have some."

Tom liked this woman. She was, in her way, a lot like Caroline. Nothing in her actions or her looks reminded him of his late wife, just the way she spoke, the way she listened when Tom spoke.

Toby was going to excuse himself and leave them alone when Doc Kreugger spotted them and came waddling over.

"Tom, just the man I been looking for," Doc

Kreugger said, doffing his hat to Katherine. "Morning Katherine, enjoying your stay?"

"Very much," Katherine answered. At least she knew one or two of the citizens of Valiant. "If you gentlemen will excuse me. Toby's wife and I have some work to do."

Katherine went inside and Tom was sorry that she had to leave. There was so much he wanted to talk to her about.

"Fine woman, that Katherine," Doc Kreugger said.

"I'll tell her that," Toby replied. "Got to get that buckskin off Josh Merkin's shod."

Toby grabbed a hoofpick and began digging away at the buckskin's hoof. He was working hard now and that left Tom to listen to whatever the doctor had to say.

"Why do you want to see me, Doc?" Tom said. "Anything I can do for you?"

Doc nodded. "There is indeed. I'm riding out to your place to take a look at Jack Madrid's arm. The marshal told me you had taken him in."

"That's so."

"How about you riding along with me? Might need you when I get there. Might not. Always good to have someone along when I check up on my patients."

Tom really wanted to ride over to Ballard's

place but he couldn't tell that to the doctor. He didn't want anyone knowing what his plans were.

"If you want me to."

"Just said as much. You ready to go now?"

"Now's as good a time as any."

They told Toby good-bye and he just grunted and nodded since he was still busy with Josh's horse.

Tom rode his mustang alongside Doc until he came to where he had tethered his horse. Doc wasn't a horseman; he actually was afraid of the animals. Still, after he had slid cautiously into the saddle he made a gallant attempt to ride with confidence. His black valise was draped around the saddle horn by its handle.

"How have you been, Tom?" Doc asked when they were on the outskirts of Valiant.

Tom shrugged. "Still getting over Caroline. It takes a while."

"Know what you mean. Seen a lot of widows and widowers in my time. They have to go one day at a time. Don't think about tomorrow, just what's ahead of them for the day."

"That's about it."

"Marshal Yoder got any ideas on who might have killed the driver and the shotgun on the stagecoach?"

"We thought it might have been someone over at Bad Falls. Turns out he was on his honeymoon when all of this happened. But Ben is still looking."

Doc Kreugger had been listening and trying to stay easy in the saddle at the same time. He looked over at Tom and said, "You got any ideas who might have done it?"

"Maybe."

"Want to talk to me about it? You know us doctors, we're like priests. Don't have to answer to anyone but the Almighty. We're as tight-lipped as they come."

Tom chewed that over in his mind, wondering if he should tell Doc Kreugger who he suspected. He had known the doctor ever since he had come to Valiant, over twelve years ago. Doc had gotten him through measles, chicken pox, and numerous broken bones and scraped shins he had accumulated during his growing-up years. Doc could be trusted.

"Been thinking a lot lately about Rune Ballard. Got some questions I would like to ask him."

"Such as?"

"Where he was when Caroline was killed. What does he know about any of this. And whatever comes to mind. Only Jack and I have been out there and Ballard wasn't home."

Doc Kreugger groaned a little as he shifted his bulk in the saddle. "He's a roamer. I hear that he goes to Laramie a lot. Sometimes Cheyenne.

Gambles, drinks too much, and Lord knows what else. One of these days he'll be ripe for Josh Merkin's business."

"That's why I want to see him. Where does he get his money? It costs a lot to go to Cheyenne and get likkered up. Far as I can see Ballard hasn't done an honest day's work since he came to Valiant."

"Go on, you're doing just fine," Doc Kreugger said, a slight smile cutting across his fleshy countenance.

" 'Bout it," Tom said, not knowing how far he should go. He was a taciturn man who didn't like to rattle on like some cowpokes he knew. Caroline and Ben Yoder were the only two people he had known that he felt free enough with to just rant on.

"So you're looking for Rune Ballard. You might be on the right track. Rune's a bad one. Only, from what I've heard, there wasn't a robbery connected with the ambush."

Tom knew that. He'd heard it somewhere, or Ben might have mentioned it.

"I figure if there wasn't a robbery then it was done for money that had already been paid."

Doc Kreugger perked up. His gray-smeared bush eyebrows rose with interest.

"You saying that somebody paid to have the

stagecoach ambushed? That's a possibility I never thought of."

"It's just an idea I came up with. I don't have no proof or nothing like that."

"I can see why you want to see Rune Ballard. He would be just the type to be a hired gunman. Wouldn't put it past him one bit."

For a time they rode in silence. Doc Kreugger didn't want to goad Tom into saying anything he would later regret. Tom was handling Caroline's death better than he had expected since they had been such a close couple when she was alive. Tom was a hard worker and had made something of that spread of land he had bought. Doc Kreugger could remember what a wild, impetuous boy Tom had been. It was some kind of a miracle his taming down after he married Caroline. A shame her being taken, nothing but a darn shame.

Tom had decided that he had said all he wanted to say to Doc. Right now he wanted in the worst way to ride over to Ballard's shanty and see if the raunchy gunslinger was home. In the distance the mountains still held their secret as to who had ambushed the stagecoach. Only the lichen-spattered rocks knew the name of the shooter. Right now he had promised the doc he would ride with him to the ranch to see how Jack was getting on. After that he'd see Rune Ballard, a promise to himself he meant to keep before the sun went down.

When they got to the ranch they tethered their horses and Jack Madrid met them at the door.

"Come to check on me, huh, Doc."

"That's what they pay me for. How you feeling, Jack? Looks to me like you are still a little puny around the gills."

"You're the doc. How do you think I feel?" Jack replied, touching the sling. He had a look of anguish on his face.

"Let's go inside and I'll check you over," Doc Kreugger said, picking up his black valise. "Come along, Tom."

Tom followed them inside where Doc Kreugger took off the sling to examine the wound. Tom went into the kitchen to get a cup of coffee. He thought it would be a good idea to leave them alone.

"I smell coffee," Doc Kreugger called out. "How about pouring me a cup?"

"Coming right up," Tom said as he reached for another mug. He took the coffee into the living room.

"It's coming along real good," Doc Kreugger said to Jack. "You just keep resting it the way you have and you won't need me poking around on it."

Tom handed the doctor his cup of coffee. Doc

Kreugger took a quick sip and put it down on the small oak coffee table.

"Long as I'm making a house call, how is that leg of yours, Tom? Having any pain?"

"Now and then. Can't say it's been bothering me any except when I ride too far."

Doc Kreugger picked up his cup and took a deep swallow. "You should be good as new in a day or two. That is if you don't decide to ride to Denver and back in one day."

"Don't have any reason to go to Denver. 'Ceptin' it would be to see my sister-in-law and her husband and new baby."

Doc Kreugger saw that he had inadvertantly stirred up painful memories and so he quickly switched the conversation. "How those Dusault boys doing anyway? If they are anything like their pa they'll turn out to be good cowpunchers."

"They are like their pa," Tom said. "Don't have to worry none when they're riding herd."

"You wouldn't have to worry none if I was fit to ride either," Jack said almost in a self-pitying way.

"Your turn will come," Tom answered and he managed a quick, quirky grin.

Doc Kreugger finished his coffee and wiped his mouth with the sleeve of his jacket. "Not bad perked coffee. Well, Madrid, you're on the mend.

Just take it easy for another day or two and you'll be back wishing you were sick again."

"Thanks, Doc," Jack said. "Appreciate you coming all the way out here for me. Guess you got your hands full with those wounded drovers in jail."

"Out of my hands," Doc said. "Marshal Yoder released them today. They're over at The Busted Nugget right now making amends."

Tom was getting anxious to ride. He wanted to see if Ballard was back from wherever it was that he had gone to. Doc Kreugger sensed that Tom was restless and made a quick exit followed by Tom.

"You do what the doc says, hear?" Tom said as he and Doc Kreugger reined their horses toward Valiant.

"Got no choice," Madrid said and watched them ride away. When they were gone he went back inside and sat down on the bed to finish his cup of coffee. Then he took out his plug of tobacco and bit off a chew. At least the doc didn't tell him he shouldn't chew.

When they got to town Doc Kreugger went his own way to check on the sick. Tom headed his mustang toward the south of town where Ballard's shack stood. It was getting on towards noon and the sun was diffused by grey storm-clouds that had swept down from the north. It was going to be a long, cold winter.

As he passed the marshal's office he looked to see if Ben was inside. His horse wasn't at the hitchrail so some problems must have come up and he was out doing his lawman's job.

Jubal Johnson was hurrying down the boardwalk to the bank but he nodded to Tom as he went on his spindly legs. As a rule Jubal didn't hurry that much. He always seemed to be a man in control of every situation. Jubal flung open and slammed shut the door to the bank as if the demons from the pit were chasing him.

Tom had other things to think about and Jubal Johnson just wasn't one of them. He had heard that Jubal had quite an arsenal of weapons that he had collected over the years. Weapons and books. He had a thirst for knowledge and, from what Tom had garnered, the good life.

By the time he had gone beyond the outskirts of Valiant, a strong, brisk wind had sprung up. Sweeping down from the peaks of the mountains, it was a portent of a brutal winter ahead.

Tom urged his horse to a gallop to cover the ground from the townsite to Ballard's place. Something inside told him that Ballard was back from wherever it was he had gone.

It was less than a mile now until he would be at Ballard's. Tom pulled out his Colt to make sure it was loaded. He didn't expect to use the gun but when it came to someone like Rune Ballard it was always wise to be prepared.

When he got to the shack he saw Rune's gray gelding sackhobbled in front of the shack. The wind had grown stronger and more intense. It whipped the rags that hung for curtains across the windows and the front door stood open.

Tom dismounted and walked cautiously to the front door. He was thankful that the wind was in his favor and he couldn't but faintly smell the garbage dump Ballard called home.

At the door Tom took out his gun and rapped the butt against the broken, slightly leaning door. He called out Rune's name and waited. There was no answer. He called Ballard's name again. Still there was an eerie silence from inside.

Cautiously Tom stepped inside. Something skittered across the floor, some rodent that vanished behind some pile of empty cans. The movement had drawn Tom's attention and there, lying on his back, his eyes staring sightlessly at him was the body of Rune Ballard.

Chapter Ten

Tom hurried over and knelt beside the body of Rune Ballard. He searched for a pulse, knowing all the while that it was a futile effort. Ballard had been dead for some time and the blood that had seeped from his head wound had begun to cake and congeal.

Slowly Tom rose to a standing position and looked around the shack. For the first time he thought of the dangerous position he had put himself in. Ballard's killer might still be in hiding somewhere in the shack.

Tom kept his Colt on the ready as he slowly gazed around the shanty. All the while he was doing this his ears were alerted to any sudden movement, to any sign that he and Ballard were not alone in the place. After carefully looking in every possible hiding place, he convinced himself that the shooter was not there any more.

Why had Ballard been shot? Tom wondered to himself. Who had killed him? Did Ballard know something he shouldn't and someone made certain he would not be able to tell a living soul? With the killing of Rune Ballard, Tom's hopes for finding the murderer of Caroline began to dwindle.

Tom's mind suddenly was not on Ballard but of trying to find Ben Yoder and let him know what happened. He backed out of the shack and didn't turn around until he felt the refreshing but chilled autumn air on his face. Tom mounted his mustang and headed back to Valiant. This would be about the third time he had gone in that direction today. Already it had been eventful. Maybe Ben was back from wherever he had gone. He had to be the one to tell him about Ballard, otherwise Ben might get the wrong idea when he heard about the killing.

Riding into Valiant, he headed straight for the marshal's office. He was relieved to see Ben's red roan gelding outside the jail.

Tom dismounted, favoring his still somewhat sore leg and rushed inside.

Ben was at his oaken desk writing with his left

hand; his arm curved in that unusual way that always was a wonder to Tom.

"Ballard's been shot," he blurted out. "He's dead."

Ben dropped the pen and got to his feet.

"Were you out there?"

Tom nodded. "I only wanted to ask him some questions. But it looks like someone beat me to it. It was a clean shot through the head."

"Tom, I told you not to do anything on your own. I know how you feel about Caroline's death. Leave it to the law."

Tom snorted. "I thought I was part of the law, being deputized and all that."

Ben walked over to Tom. "Sorry, I clean forgot. Better go have a look-see at Ballard. Want to ride along?"

"Might as well. I've already cut a fresh trail from Valiant to his place."

They spurred their horses into a mean gallop and covered the distance from Valiant to Ballard's in hardly any time. When they got there Ben and Tom went inside.

"Lord, what a smell!" Ben said after he entered the shack.

"Ballard wasn't the best housekeeper," Tom said ironically.

"That how you found him?"

"Lying there. Looks to me like maybe he might

have been expecting someone and he turned to the door. That's when he was shot."

"That's the way I see it too," Ben said.

"Now I guess the next question is who did it?" Tom said. "I kinda was hoping Ballard might shed some light on the ambush. Way I see it, this is all connected."

Ben nodded. "Looks that way. And then again Ballard rubbed skin the wrong way on a lot of mean hombres. Could have been someone who was bent on getting even."

Tom hadn't thought of that. He had been thinking along one trail and never given any thought to another.

"It could have happened that way. Only I got this feelin' Ballard was in some way mixed up in the ambush."

"Now we'll never know," Ben said. "Let's go outside. I need a breath of fresh air."

"I'm with you on that score."

They both made a hasty exit. Outside they took big gulps of air into their lungs.

"Can't figure out how a man can live that way," Ben said quietly. "Darn near like an animal."

"Animals are cleaner," were Tom's feelings.

As they stood outside the shack, a burst of wind swept by. It was cold and smelled of rain.

But it was welcome. Anything to clear away the vestiges of their exposure to Ballard's shebang.

"We'll have to tell Josh Merkin that he's got some work out here. Probably have to bury him and that miner from the stagecoach in potter's field."

Tom squinted at Ben as a new wave of dusty wind bruised his face. "Never did find out who the old man was?"

"No trace. Like Ballard he must have not had any living relatives. Or at least any relatives who would want to claim them. Thought for a while I recognized him, but I was on the wrong trail."

"What about the other hombre? The well-dressed one? Anything on him?"

"Still waiting to hear from Cheyenne. You'd think somebody like him would be missed. There was a man in on the Denver stage who was asking questions about the ambush, so I heard. He was pretty well-dressed too. Wanted to know if we had a bank in town. Someone sent him over to see Jubal. Last I heard he was put up at the Brewer's Hotel."

Tom was very interested in anything that had to do with Caroline's killing.

"Get his name?"

"Oscar something . . . let's see . . . Oscar Sheldon, that's it," Ben said. "Why you askin'?"

"Just curious. Don't get that many strangers

here in Valiant these days. You want me to see Merkin about takin' care of Ballard?"

Ben looked at the papers piled high on the oaken desk and smiled at Tom. "Would be beholden to you if you would."

"Leave it to me. Looks like you got your work cut out for you for another month there on your desk."

"Maybe you bein' deputy I ought to give you all the paperwork to do."

"I'm leavin' before you really mean that," Tom said and walked quickly out the door. He glanced back as he was closing the door to see Ben scratching his head as he looked at the small mountain of papers on his desk.

Tom headed for Merkin's Barber Shop and Funeral Parlor, which was just down the street from the jailhouse. Josh Merkin was not what you would expect a funeral director to look like. He was a short, rotund man with florid, deep-veined jowls. Joshua Merkin was a man who liked a good drink and a good joke. There was always a bottle of Kentucky sour-mash close by whenever he wasn't shaving and barbering or fixing a corpse to look as natural as possible.

Today Josh was in a good mood. After all it had been a financially profitable week for him. If this kept up he might be able to retire and take that trip to San Francisco he'd always dreamed about. He longed for those full-bodied women he'd seen in magazines and billboards when he took an occasional buying trip to Laramie or Cheyenne. Yes, siree, if business was as good as this week then it was *adios* Valiant and a rip-snortin' hello to the City By The Bay.

Josh glanced up from polishing the handles on a casket just as Tom Cardy came into the shop. Josh hoped that Tom wasn't there to ask for any kind of a rebate on the funeral he'd handled for Tom's wife. If he was, the answer was going to be a flat, no-two-ways-about-it, no.

"Afternoon, Tom," Josh said in his best business voice. Looking up at Tom, the wattles around his neck bobbed up and down like rubber rings. "What can I do for you?"

"Not for me but Rune Ballard. Been shot in the head. Marshal Yoder and I found him a little while ago in his shack."

Josh put on his best professional look of sorrow. "Rest the poor man's soul. I'll get to him right away. You said he was in his shack?"

Tom didn't like being in the undertaking parlor; it brought back too many sad memories. He just wanted to get this over with and head for the Brewer's Hotel.

"That's right. Been dead for a spell. Think you can handle it?"

Josh rose to the occasion. "My good man,

that's what I'm trained to do. Merkin's Barber Shop and Funeral Parlor are up to any occasion. My father was a mortician and his father before that. Undertaking has been in the Merkin blood for over two decades."

"Good. Thanks, Mr. Merkin. I knew we could depend on you." Tom started to leave.

"Oh, Mr. Cardy, who is paying for the funeral?"

"Ask the Marshal. He said he'd be buried in potter's field." Tom was almost pleased to see the woebegone look on Josh Merkin's face.

"Does the Marshal think I'm in this business for my health?"

"You argue with Marshal Yoder about that. Good day, Mr. Merkin."

"It was," Josh said but Tom had already gone out and shut the door behind him.

Tom was glad that was over. Josh Merkin might grumble and grouse about being paid but you could always count on him for a first-rate piece of business.

Still Tom was glad to leave the Barbershop and Funeral Parlor and shuck off the memories of when he had last needed Merkin's services.

The Brewer's Hotel was built on the corner of Main Street and Aspen. It was a two-storied brick building and it was the newest structure in Valiant. An alley ran behind the building and most of the tenants preferred staying on the first floor or second with a view of the street.

Tom stood in front of the building looking up at the sign that creaked and swayed in the late autumn wind. He had been in the hotel many times. When he and Caroline were about to have their wedding, they rented some rooms for Caroline's sister and brother-in-law and some out-of-town friends.

They had held a dinner party for the members of the wedding in the plush, heavily carpeted dining room. Ben had come and he had sat at the same table with Tom and Caroline. There had been a lot of joshing and good food and even some dancing with the accompaniment of two fiddlers from Bad Falls.

It was now getting late in the afternoon. The sun was edging its way toward the western horizon. The Brewer's Hotel was still brightly lighted on one side and in dim shadows on the other side. By now the alley behind the hotel would be even more in shadows and a place to be avoided after sundown.

Reminding himself why he had come to the hotel, Tom took off his Stetson, ran his hand over his light brown hair, and tugged at his jacket. The Brewer was a pretty elegant place and Tom felt he owed it that much courtesy.

Tom walked over and entered the building. He

found himself in the lobby. Overhead gleaming brass lamps cast a soft light from the chandelier. The lobby had one or two people milling about and there was a man asleep on a horsehair sofa, a magazine open on his lap, and he was lightly snoring in a way that would be approved of in The Brewer.

For a few moments Tom was back in time. Back to the day when he had first come into the Brewer. The dining room was to his right and Tom ambled over to peer inside. It was just as he had remembered it. The tables were swathed in white linen tablecloths and the carefully polished silverware sparkled in the light cast by the wagon-wheeled chandeliers. He glanced at the small raised wooden stage where the fiddlers had once stood and he could even hear the music they played. Brewer's Hotel had a coal furnace and the guests all dressed up in their best for dinner. It was an elegant place all right. The guests dined on expensive viands, everything from caviar to peaches floating in champagne.

It was all there, and yet it wasn't. Tom had to almost shake himself to realize he was slipping into the past, a past that was where it should be and he had no right to bring it up. Not at this moment in time.

Tom turned away from the dining room and walked across the lobby to the front desk. Arley

Williams was sorting through some papers but he glanced up when he saw Tom. Arley and Tom had gone to school together but Arley wasn't as close to Tom as Ben was. Arley was a nice man, quiet and slightly near-sighted. He wore wire-rimmed glasses that made his face seem like he was all eyes.

"Tom Cardy! How you been?" Arley said. "Sorry to hear about Caroline. Terrible, terrible thing. They caught whoever did it yet? Do they know why they done it? And what's going to be done about it?"

Tom smiled at Arley. "Lots of questions, Arley. Which one you want answered first?"

Arley grinned. He had always been the one in class who was never satisfied with an answer. Always just another question from Arley Williams was what the class expected.

"All of them."

"I'm getting along pretty good. Takes a while to get over something like this."

Arley's smile faded. He put aside the papers he had been sorting. "Me and Cloris should have you over for supper one of these nights, Tom. Just didn't know if you were up to it."

"Nice of you, Arley. I'll think about that. Had a few offers like that lately. Mrs. Dusault's been bringing food over for me and Jack Madrid."

Arley always listened with his mouth wide

open. "Jack Madrid stayin' out at the ranch? Did I hear he got shot up at the Nugget?"

"Took it in his arm. But Doc Kreugger's been tendin' to him. Jack'll be riding in a couple of days."

Arley closed his mouth. "Always did like Jack. He's sort of a loner but not squirrelly like a lot of them drover's who ride alone."

Tom didn't want to pursue this anymore. Jack was his friend and he didn't like talking about his friends; in a good or bad way.

"Arley, can I ask a favor?"

"Name it."

"You got a man registered here name of Sheldon? Came in on today's stage from Denver."

Arley nodded.

"Oscar Sheldon. Speaking of someone who plays it close to his vest, that's this Sheldon dude. He doesn't talk much. Only asked where the bank was, that was it."

"Is he in?"

Arley nodded once more. "Think so. He went out just after he checked in. Came back and, as far as looks go, was mad as a scalded hornet. Went right to his room."

"Mad? Any idea why?"

Arley shrugged. "Must have been something he saw or learned at the bank. Only thing I can figure."

Tom asked Arley which room Oscar Sheldon was in and was told room five.

"Ground floor?"

"Right. One with only one window and that's facing the alley. Guess Mr. Sheldon doesn't want any company. But I guess it's okay if you go, Tom. Seeing as how you are a lawman now."

Tom raised an eyebrow. "How did you know I was deputized?"

"Valiant has no secrets," Arley said. "Not with someone like Elva Kleindorf around."

"Elva knows things even before they happen."

"And she tells Jubal about all of them."

Tom shook his head as he strolled down the shadowy hallway toward Oscar Sheldon's room. It was quiet in the hallway and when Tom found the room he hesitated before rapping on the door. He was thinking about what he would say to this man. Did he know anything about the ambush or was he just a businessman who happened to be asking innocent questions about what happened at Devil's Whip?

Taking a deep breath, Tom knocked on the door. He waited. This Oscar Sheldon must be a real quiet person; Tom couldn't hear a sound from the other side of the door.

Tom rapped again, this time louder and longer. Still there was no answer. Tom reached out and touched the doorknob and tried it. It was locked.

Shrugging, Tom went back down the hallway to the front desk.

"He must have gone out again," Tom said.

Arley looked puzzled. "Couldn't have. He had to pass this desk if he did. Only he didn't. I swear. I been here all the time. Think maybe he's asleep?"

Tom shook his head. "Dunno. If he is he's a mighty hard pillow pounder. Couldn't rouse him."

Arley frowned. "Don't think something's happened to him, do you?"

Tom just turned his head and glanced back down the hallway toward Oscar Sheldon's room.

"Maybe we'd better check on him," Arley said, grabbing a metal ring of master keys. "You come with me, Tom?"

Tom nodded his agreement and tacit support to Arley's question and followed the lanky, loose-limbed clerk down the hallway. First Arley knocked loudly and firmly on the door. "Desk clerk, Mr. Sheldon."

He waited for a second or two but the occupant of room five failed to respond.

Arley turned to look at Tom for another brief second before he inserted the key in the lock.

"Here goes something I hope doesn't get me fired," were Arley's final words as he cautiously opened the door. There was no sound from within the room but Tom could sense there was someone there. Why that someone didn't answer the door they soon found out.

"Oh, my God!" Arley groaned in a sick, failing voice.

Tom walked over to the overstuffed chair where the late Oscar Sheldon had been sitting with his back to the window. His face was a bluish, bloated death mask. Tom tried to undo the thin, corded rope that had garroted the man. He felt for a pulse but knew that Oscar Sheldon was no longer among the living.

"Is he dead?" Arley moaned. "What'll we do?"

Tom's hands were shaking slightly but he steadied them. One of the two of them had to remain calm.

"Go get Ben," Tom said in as cool, controlled a voice as he could muster. "Tell him what happened."

Arley was more than eager to get out of the room. "Right. I'll get Ben. What about you?"

"I'll stay here and wait until you get back."

Arley started for the door but dropped the ring of master keys. It was the only sound in the room.

"Tom? Who did it? Who do you think did it?"

"Don't know. Right now, Arley, you get a move on."

Arley walked sideways to the door. He took

one final gander at Oscar Sheldon and shuddered before he hurried out of the room.

Now that Arley was gone Tom glanced around the room. Drawers were pulled out from the chests and hung in an askew manner. Oscar Sheldon from his appearance did not look like the sort of man who was sloppy about his clothing. There was an open brown valise on the bed. The contents had been scattered all over the cotton bedspread and the floor.

Someone had been looking for something after they had killed Sheldon. He must have been sitting in the chair by the window when the killer had entered through that same way and strangled him. Tom just knew that it all tied in with the ambush at Devil's Whip. Who was Oscar Sheldon and what was he doing in Valiant? If he knew the anser to that he would know who killed Caroline and the others.

Tom quickly went through the papers on the bed. They were just documents that he couldn't understand. He did, however, see one name that stood out. That paper he folded neatly and shoved into his back pants pocket.

After that Tom went back to the body of Oscar Sheldon. He managed to get the rope untied just as he heard voices coming down the hallway. It had to be Arley with Ben Yoder.

"He hadn't gone out . . . Tom came to see him

. . . he couldn't wake him . . . I got the master key . . . we found him."

By this time they were at the door to the room. Ben stepped inside but said to Arley, "You go back to your work, Arley. For now just go on like nothin's happened. Can you do that?"

"I'll try, Ben," he said as he gratefully turned and hurried down the hallway to his desk.

"How did it happen?" Ben asked.

Tom held up the piece of rope. "Strangled, by this. Whoever did it came through that open window. The door to the room was locked from the inside. It had to have happened that way."

Ben came over and knelt beside the body, looking at it for a minute. Then he stood up and said, "What were you doing here? And who is this man?"

"Oscar Sheldon. I was just going to ask him some questions."

"About Devil's Whip?"

"Right."

"Seems to me someone else had some questions that Mr. Sheldon didn't want to answer."

Tom waited for Ben to get angry and tell him to lay off this personal crusade. But he didn't. Instead he said, "Guess maybe you'd better go see Josh Merkin again. We'll be needin' his services once more."

"I'm on my way."

Tom started toward the door. Ben caught him by the arm. "And come back when you get through. We got to question the people who were staying here at the Brewer."

Tom just nodded and Ben released his grip. Tom walked out of the room and down the shadowy hallway.

Chapter Eleven

Tom kept his word when he left the Brewer. He rode his black mustang over to Merkin's and told Josh what had happened.

"What's going on around here? This keeps up and Valiant will turn into a ghost town," Josh grumbled as he put his black jacket on. Secretly Josh was rather curious to see who this feller was what got himself killed at the Brewer. Nice place like that, this could put a dent in its reputation.

"You going over there now?" Tom asked.

"On my way."

"Tell Marshal Yoder I'll be there shortly," Tom said as he mounted his horse.

"I'll do that little thing," Merkin said as he slammed the door to his funeral parlor and climbed aboard his buckboard that served as the city's hearse.

Tom waited until Merkin had gee-uped the horses and had headed the rig for the Brewer before reining his own horse toward the outskirts of town. He had to pass the marshal's office and the bank as he trotted down the main street. Ben was at the hotel so all was quiet at the jail and there was no sign of life at the bank either.

Tom put things together as he spurred his horse into a faster trot when he got to the outskirts of Valiant. The ambush, the shooting of Gordy Witcher and Red Bobbins. The spooking of the team of horses and the stagecoach crashing down the side of the mountain. Ultimately, the deaths of the passengers inside the stagecoach. His Caroline being one of the passengers.

With these thoughts in mind and a remembered face outside The Busted Nugget after the shootout Tom began to draw the loose ends together. It wouldn't be a hangman's noose, that Tom would take care of. Hanging would be too swift, too easy. Tom had other ideas on vengeance.

There was a well-beaten trail beyond Valiant that led to Jubal Johnson's house. In the past Tom had passed by the house many times. He had wondered what it was like inside. He was soon to find out. After all, hadn't Jubal himself given him an invite to come out? Tom was just being neighborly, just being civilized, and curious.

Tom got off his gelding at the front of Johnson's home. There was a rig with a team of horses near the front door. Hastily stacked inside the wagon were boxes and clothes and two red crystal lamps.

As Tom stood there Jubal came hurrying out of the house carrying an armload of shirts. When he saw Tom, Jubal almost dropped the shirts he was carrying.

"Afternoon, Jubal," Tom said casually. He smiled at the banker, who was looking at Tom with eyes filled with a mixture of fear and furtiveness.

Composing himself Jubal said, "Why, Tom, what brings you out here?"

"Thought I'd pay you a visit. Just being neighborly. But I see you're busy."

Jubal hadn't moved from where he had abruptly halted. One of the fine, monogrammed linen shirts slid away from the heap and drifted down, landing lightly in the dust.

"Let me help you," Tom said, moving forward and picking up the fallen shirt. "Looks like you're getting ready to pull up stakes. And in a hurry."

Tom draped the shirt over the others on Jubal's arm and at this distance he looked directly into the banker's eyes. Jubal's lips were moving but no sounds came out. Tom's smile was still on his lips but there was no friendliness in his eyes.

"Better put those in the rig, Jubal. Maybe I can just help you with these."

Tom took the shirts gently but firmly from Jubal and twisted his torso so that it was no effort to put the shirts in the wagon.

"Mind telling me where you are headed, Jubal?" Tom rested his hand on the butt of his Colt .45. This gesture did not go unnoticed by the banker.

Jubal swallowed hard. A row of sweat sprang out above his upper lip. He was breathing hard and his hands were shaking almost imperceptibly.

"Just a little trip," Jubal said and wiped the sweat away from his lip with the sleeve of his shirt. "Been planning on it for some time. Now is as good as any to get away."

Tom glanced at the rig and then back to Jubal. "Taking a lot of things for just a trip, ain't you?"

Jubal suddenly swallowed hard and said, "I've got a lot of work to do, Tom. Maybe we can talk some other time. Excuse me."

Jubal turned abruptly and walked inside. Tom was right behind him.

"Don't know if there will be another time," Tom said as Jubal moved from the short hallway into the living room. Tom couldn't help but notice the deep, plush carpeting throughout the house. There were paintings in oil decorating the walls and the furniture must have cost Jubal quite a passel of money.

"Did you know there was a man in town from Denver?" Tom said. "He has something to do with banks. Name he goes by is Oscar Sheldon."

Jubal's back was to him but Tom could see the muscles in his shoulders tighten as Jubal said, "Don't believe I've met the man."

"Funny thing," Tom said in the same even, taunting voice, "I was told he went to the bank to see you. Just today."

Jubal walked over to a bookcase that lined an entire wall. Tom had never seen so many books in his entire life. Jubal took down a few books to pack away.

"I must have missed him. As you can see, I've been getting ready for my trip."

"Too bad you missed him. Don't think you'll get a chance now."

Jubal studied the binding on a book. "Why is that?"

"We found him dead at the Brewer today. Somebody killed him."

Jubal didn't flinch or show any sign of emotion. In a way Tom had to admire the way Jubal had gotten control of himself. He was a cold-blooded killer and what he had done just didn't seem to bother him. Not now anyway. When he had first confronted Jubal it had been a different story.

"I'm sorry to hear that. Did they find out who killed him?"

"I think I know who did it."

"If you know then why don't you turn him in to Marshal Yoder?"

Tom walked over to the bookcase. "I don't have to do that. Now that I've been deputized. I can make the arrest myself. But then you know I'm a deputy. Elva Kleindorf must have told you."

"Possibly."

"Elva tells you lots of things, don't she?" Tom's hand ran down the spines of the books. "Like maybe how I was going to see Rune Ballard."

"I don't know what you're talking about," Jubal's voice was betraying him. Tom knew he was slowly chipping away at the banker's false front.

"Again a funny thing. Rune Ballard is dead too. Somebody shot him up close. Probably with a derringer. Sort of like one of those you got hangin' on your wall."

"Why don't you come out and say what you came here for?" Jubal said, turning to put the books he was holding into a box.

"I thought I'd been doin' a pretty decent job of that. You got any ideas who might have killed that Sheldon man? And while you're at it, who wanted to do away with Ballard?"

Jubal walked over and took down a few more books. His hands were visibly shaking now.

"You'd better be careful making accusations you can't prove, Deputy," Jubal said in a scoffing voice.

Tom's hand stopped at a book that caught his eye. He pulled it slowly away from the bookshelf. Quietly Tom glanced at the title then opened the book to the last page.

"I didn't know you were interested in first editions, Deputy," Jubal said mockingly. "As a matter of fact I didn't know you could read."

Tom held up the book. "Where did you get this?"

Jubal put the books he was holding in the crook of his arm. Then he walked over to Tom. When he saw what Tom was holding he halted.

"Bullwer-Lytton . . . I . . . I don't remember. I must have picked it up somewhere."

Tom's fist came up with such force it smashed Jubal's nose before sending him crashing against the far wall. "My nose! My nose! You've broken my nose! I'm bleeding!"

Tom went for his Colt .45 and it leaped from its holster into his steady, practiced hand.

"Get up, Johnson. Stand up. You ain't hurtin' nearly as bad as you're going to."

Slowly, awkwardly Jubal got to his feet. He was holding his nose with one hand. Blood had gushed down through his fingers and was staining his white, monogrammed shirt.

"Now, tell me where you got this book! Or maybe I'll tell you. You got it from my wife's dead body. I gave her this book before she went to Denver. Here, on the last page, is my mark. You stole this book after you had my wife killed."

Jubal was weaving. The pain from the broken nose was making him sick to his stomach.

"Am I right? You paid Ballard to ambush the stagecoach, didn't you."

Jubal just painfully lowered and raised his head. His eyes were like a trapped animal frantically searching for a way out after being cornered.

"Why? Not just for a book? You can't make me believe that. Not for one ringtailed second."

Jubal spoke through the fingers of the hand across his nose and mouth.

"It all started a few years ago. I needed some money. So I did something to the accounting books. I meant to pay it back. But I needed some more. Before I knew it I had gotten in deeper and deeper."

Tom held the Colt .45 steady and the book tightly in the other hand.

"Then I got a letter from a bank inspector in Denver. He was coming to go over the books. I couldn't let that happen, don't you understand? I could lose all this. It's my life. I just couldn't lose it. Maybe go to prison. I hired Ballard to stop the stagecoach. If your wife got killed I'm sorry about that. But I have my future to think about."

Tom resisted the impulse to pull the trigger. It took all his willpower to not raise the Colt and smash Johnson's skull. Controlling himself, Tom said, "Go on. I want all of it."

"The examiner was killed in the ambush. That gave me time to get things together. I've made plans to go to Mexico. I have the money in a carpetbag."

"What about Oscar and Ballard?"

Jubal was like a dammed-up river that had suddenly broken free of its boundaries. He gasped for air as he told Tom all about what had happened.

"Ballard wanted more money. He threatened to tellin' what had happened. He may not have if he was sober but he drank too much. Was too loose with his mouth. I had to get rid of him."

Tom moved just slightly so that he would have a better vantage point. "Elva told you that I was coming out to see Ballard, right?"

Jubal nodded. "She overheard you talking to Madrid outside The Busted Nugget. Elva never keeps anything to herself. So I just got there ahead of you. Made sure that Ballard wouldn't talk anymore."

"This Sheldon, he was here to find out what happened to the other examiner."

Again Jubal nodded. "He came to the bank, asking questions. I told him I hadn't seen the man. Then he wanted to look over the accounts. I told him to come back in the morning. He didn't like it but he went away."

Tom watched the blood drip through Jubal's fingers. It should have bothered him but he felt nothing towards the man.

"I left the bank and followed him to the hotel. He'd told me which room he was in. I went down the alley. I saw him sit down with his back to the window. The window was open and I found a piece of rope lying in the alley. He didn't hear me come in. He didn't put up much of a fight."

"Then you went through his things."

"Anything that might incriminate me. I needed a little more time. After I got to Mexico I would get lost and nobody would be able to find me."

"Ballard must have been the one who took those potshots at Madrid and me when we were on the Devil's Whip."

"Could have been. Ballard did a lot of foolish things, when he got liquored up. He might have gone up to the Whip to see if he could find any gold or valuables that were overlooked."

Tom looked around for the first time. Really looked at the fine house Jubal Johnson lived in. But he had paid for all this with the money from people in the valley.

"Too bad you won't be able to make that trip," Tom said.

"I need to see a doctor," Jubal wailed. "I think my nose is broken."

"That'll have to wait. Right now you're coming along with me."

Tom turned his head for a moment to take a final look at the plush living quarters. It was what Jubal had been waiting for. He gave Tom a shove that caught him off guard. Tom tripped over some crates and fell.

Jubal ran to the gun rack on the wall and clawed at a Springfield with blood-smeared hands. He had almost gotten the rifle out when Tom slammed his Colt against Jubal's hand. The sound of bones smashing and Jubal's screams of pain filled the house.

Tom grabbed Jubal by the collar and dragged him across the room and out of the house. He had to drop Caroline's book in order to do this but he knew where to find it when he later needed to.

"Get on," Tom said, pointing his six-shooter at the buckboard. "Climb up."

Using his good hand Jubal obediently and painfully lifted his body to the rider's side of the buckboard. Tom went around to the other side and got aboard. With one hand he grabbed the reins and smacked the rumps of the horses. The team trotted away, their hot breaths steaming the cool, nippy air.

There was no sound between the two men but that of Jubal who made a whimpering noise as he clutched his broken hand with his good one. The bleeding had stopped on his nose as it caked like a scarlet mole outside of one nostril.

Tom put his Colt .45 on his lap where he could get to it with ease. He didn't think Jubal would try anything from the condition he was in.

Tom headed the buckboard away from the trail that led to Valiant. They had only gone a short distance when Jubal noticed the departure.

"This isn't the way to Valiant. Where are you taking me? I got to see a doctor."

Tom said nothing. He kept his eyes on the mountains which grew closer and closer with each turning of the wagon's wheels.

"Look, Tom," Jubal muttered. "You got to tell me where you're headed. I know you don't approve of me. But if you take me back to the house and turn your back on what you know, I'll make it worth your while."

All Tom did was give Jubal a look that gave him an unspoken answer to his plea.

Jubal continued to moan as he pulled his shirt as close to his shaking body as he could. In the distance Tom saw a lone rider approaching. Tom reached into the back of the buckboard and grabbed one of Jubal's shirts. He put it in his lap covering the Colt.

"I've got this gun aimed right at your gut, Jubal. You say one word you shouldn't and you'll be suckin' air through your gut. Understand?"

Jubal shifted in the seat and said, "I understand."

The rider turned out to be Andy Dusault. He hailed Tom with a wave of his hand.

"Tom and Jubal, *bonjour*."

"Good to see you, Andy. Your boys are doing a fine job on the range."

Andy, whose wind-burned face was always either smiling or getting ready to, beamed with parental pride.

"They do their best, Tom. Are you feeling all right, Jubal? You look a little piqued."

Jubal, who had hid his battered nose with his good hand, just nodded.

"Jubal is a little puny today, Andy. But he'll be all right. Where you bound for?"

"Back to my spread. Had some business to take care of in Bad Falls. On my way home to some good French cookin' and to see *mon petit chouchou.*"

Tom smiled at the good-natured Frenchman. He had never known Andy to ever raise his voice or get angry at anyone, particularly his wife and boys.

"Had a little excitement over at Bad Falls. Marshal over there told me there was a killing."

Tom cocked an eyebrow. "How's that?"

"A feller got bushwhacked. Shot clean out of the saddle. Town didn't seem too upset about it. Seems the drover wasn't too well liked."

Tom held the shirt on his lap more tightly as a cold wind blowing down from the snow-capped mountains swept over them. "Who got it?"

"Feller owned the local mercantile. Name of Gadsen. George Gadsen."

Tom felt that what goes around comes around. Gadsen got maybe what he deserved. "Don't surprise me none."

"Know this Gadsen?"

Tom shrugged. "Met him once. Didn't take to him."

"Left a wider. But she'll be well off. Got a house fit for a queen and a mercantile business and lots of golden eagles had been stashed away at the mansion."

With another blast of wind Andy shivered and said, "Better get on my way. Looks like a storm's on the way. Afternoon, Tom . . . Jubal."

Andy touched his hat brim, then spurred his stallion and rode away in the direction of Valiant. After he had gone Tom gee-uped the team and continued on his mission.

By the time they reached the road that led to Devil's Whip, the mountains were deep in purple and dark grays. Through a rift in the clouds a feeble sun sent a shaft of light across the buckboard. Jubal moved so that he could absorb all the warmth he could from the paucity of light.

"I got a jacket back there. Can I get it?" Jubal asked.

"Where is it?" Tom asked, keeping his eye on the road and the team.

"Just behind you," Jubal said. "Please, I'm freezing to death."

Tom reached behind himself and felt for the jacket. It was beneath some shirts that he just tossed carelessly aside. Then he tossed the jacket to Jubal, who slipped it on and looked miserable.

"You're the law, Tom Cardy," Jubal said. "You got to take me in. You can't abuse a prisoner."

"Know a lot about how people should be treated, don't you," Tom said in a voice that was as cold as the keening wind.

Jubal didn't say anything more. His hand was beginning to swell and turn purple. It hurt so bad that he tried not to move it.

Tom watched Jubal out of the corner of his eye. He could see how miserable and pain-ridden the banker was. He should have felt sorry for him. If it had been anyone else but Jubal Johnson he would have. But now that they were nearing Devil's Whip Caroline's death came rushing back to him. He saw her face, the frightened look in her distorted features. He saw the stagecoach and the other passengers inside. Even though he hadn't been there, had been spared that experience by Ben Yoder, Tom could imagine what it all had looked like.

"It's getting dark," Jubal finally said. "We shouldn't be on this road when it gets dark. No tellin' what can happen to us."

"No telling," Tom said ominously.

"This is Devil's Whip, isn't it?" Jubal said. "You're taking me to Devil's Whip. I know this place."

"You should. You were up here with Ballard, weren't you? Did you hide behind some of those outcroppings?"

Jubal couldn't stop himself. Talking was better than all this silence. He had to keep Tom talking. He couldn't stand the silence and the wind.

"Ballard was right in front of me. He used his

rifle. I hadn't expected the horses to spook the way they did. I hadn't expected the stagecoach to go over the side. What I had planned was just to get rid of the bank examiner."

Tom could still see plainly ahead. They were nearing the place where the stagecoach had gone over the side of the mountain. He remembered the spot when he and Madrid had been there.

Tom pulled hard on the reins and coaxed the team into stopping.

Tom sat there for a minute looking first at Jubal and then at the still broken underbrush and deep slashing rut where the stagecoach had gone over the side.

Finally he turned to Jubal and said, "Out."

Jubal thought he hadn't heard right. He looked at Tom and said, "What did you say?"

"I said, out," Tom repeated. "Out right now."

Chapter Twelve

Jubal got out of the buckboard. The wind whipped his hair into his eyes and he was hunched over in a desperate attempt to keep warm.

"You going to shoot me?" he cried out in a voice that was raw and hoarse.

Tom slapped the reins of the team and the buckboard startled to amble away.

Jubal ran over to the buckboard. "You aren't going to leave me here! You can't do that! I'll freeze to death. I'll die up here."

Jubal had grabbed with his good hand the side of the buckboard. "Don't do this. You're a lawman now. You can't do this."

Tom reached over with his booted left foot and

pressed down hard on Jubal's clutching fingers. With a cry of agony Jubal let go. He was swearing now. Every word that he had ever heard in his short life that took the Lord's name in vain and questioned Tom's rightful birth came pouring out of his mouth.

"I'll get out of here! I swear I will! I'll get you for this Tom Cardy! I'll get you for this!"

The wind was at a full gale by now, drowning out the futile cries of Jubal Johnson. Rain, mixed with sleet, pelted Tom's face and he pulled his coat closer for warmth. When the wind quieted for a moment or two Tom could hear the cries of Jubal Johnson. He tried not to let it get to him.

Look what Johnson had done to Caroline. To Gordy Witcher, to Red Robbins and the others. Didn't he deserve what he was getting? He had killed Ballard and Sheldon himself. The man was no more than a self-educated animal. He had been a robber, in a way, of other people's money. He had lived on the blood, sweat, and tears of honest investors in the bank. What he was getting, he deserved.

Tom tried the best he could to put Jubal out of his mind. Things were different out here in the West, in Wyoming. You had to make your own law, you had to protect yourself and your family.

But it wasn't working for Tom. Maybe it was that he kept seeing Caroline's face and hearing what she had said around the kitchen table or later when they were sitting together, his arms holding her tightly.

Would this be the way Caroline would want him to handle this? Would this be the way she would want her death to be avenged? Tom said 'yes' to the wailing wind. But he knew in his heart he meant the opposite.

Tom pulled back on the reins and the team came to a halt. By now the rain was coming down in great, silver-colored shafts. He was getting soaked to the skin and he knew Jubal was even worse.

"Great! Let him die of pneumonia!" he yelled at the rain and wind. "I ain't going back to him. He deserves what he's getting."

His words seemed to stick to his lips as the wind whipped across them. He looked over his shoulder at Devil's Whip. The road was dark and menacing. The demons from the pit were back there. They were doing their work on Jubal Johnson.

Without another word Tom turned the team around and headed back in the direction he had come. The bitterness that was in his mouth began to fade away. He found that he was breathing more easily and he felt peaceful in his gut.

Ahead of him, through the driving wind and

rain, he saw Jubal stumbling and almost crawling down the road like a drowning rat.

By the time Tom got the buckboard to him, Jubal had collapsed and fallen into a mud bank. Tom got out of the rig and sloshed through the mud to Jubal. He knelt down and lifted the man up. Jubal's nose had started to bleed again and it was covered with a mixture of blood and mountain dirt.

Tom half carried, half dragged Jubal to the wagon. Somehow with a lot of pushing and pulling he got the rain-soaked banker onto the seat. There were a few blankets in the back and Tom pulled them out and wound them around Jubal.

Jubal opened his eyes for the first time and saw Tom. He didn't thank him but there was a strange, crooked smile on his lips. "I knew you wouldn't leave me there, Lawman," he said.

Tom just shook his head and said, "If it weren't for that and my Caroline I'd gladly leave you there to be wolf-bait."

Then Tom set course for Valiant. By the time they reached the end of Devil's Whip the rain had turned to fine snow. Tom was cold and uncomfortable. He really didn't care how Jubal felt. He had done all he could for the man, more than he had wanted to. If he didn't survive the trip to Valiant it wouldn't be his fault.

Jubal sat huddled beneath the blankets and

every once in a while he would mutter something. Something that only he could understand. Tom stopped paying any attention to the miscreant. Right now he just wanted to get to Valiant, turn his captive over to Ben Yoder, and get back to the ranch for some warming hot coffee.

He saw the lights of Valiant in the distance and came out of his stupor. He had turned everything and everyone off while they rode the last few miles to town. Tom had no idea what time it was but he knew it would be late, probably after two in the morning.

There were a few lights blazing in the windows of the stores and some houses as he urged the team of horses down the main street of Valiant.

When he came to the jailhouse he tethered the team and hurried to the door. He opened it and went quickly inside. It was warm and almost took his breath away. Tom went right away to the back room which was Ben Yoder's quarters.

"Ben! Ben!" He yelled at the sleeping man in bed. "Get up. It's me, Tom. I gotta talk to you."

Ben made some sort of noise like a bear being awakened during winter hibernation. He threw the blanket away and stood up in his long johns. Ben rubbed his eyes and yawned. "What the hell! What time is it?"

"Don't know," Tom said. "I got our man outside. I got the man who killed Ballard and that bank examiner from Denver."

"Wait 'til I get my drawers on," Ben said, reaching for his denim pants and a flannel shirt. He pulled on his boots and then ran a hand through his wiry, dark hair.

"Where is this hombre?" he said in a voice that was still heavy with sleep.

"Outside in his rig," Tom said and he walked ahead of the marshal. Tom shook his head showering rain water around him.

"You're wet to the skin. Where you been?" Ben said when they came to the light of the office. "What's going on here?"

"Tell you later. Right now we'd better get our prisoner inside."

When Ben saw who it was he turned to Tom and said, "Are you loco! That's Jubal Johnson out there. Look at him!"

"I know who it is and that's the man who pulled the trigger on Ballard and strangled Oscar Sheldon. He confessed to me tonight."

"Let's get him inside," Ben said as he reached across the rig to take hold of the shivering banker.

Together the two men got Jubal inside and Ben sat him down and poured a cup of coffee for him. Tom helped himself. Jubal cupped the hot coffee in trembling hands.

"Look at him!" Ben said again. "What happened to his nose? And that hand?"

"Tried to pull a gun on me. It was self-defense."

Jubal was in no condition to say anything. Ben told Tom to wait there while he fetched Doc Kreugger. Jubal still hadn't said a word. His mind had long since cut itself off from the rest of his miserable body. He just automatically drank from the cup but he didn't show any reaction.

When Doc Kreugger got there he shook his head and went to work. After he had fixed the nose and bandaged the hand he said, "No more midnight calls, Marshal. Even I got to get my rest."

"I promise, Doc," Ben said. "And thanks."

Ben and Tom put Jubal to bed in one of the bunks inside a cell. Then Ben locked the door and together he and Tom went back to the office.

"Want to tell me everything?" Ben asked when they had gotten back.

Tom took a big swallow from his cup and then told Ben the whole story. How he had suspected Jubal when he found the slip of paper in Sheldon's room with the banker's name on it. How he had found the book in Jubal's library and how he remembered Elva being outside The Busted Nugget before Ballard had been shot.

When he finished Ben said, "He'll get a fair

trial. I'll try to explain to the judge about you taking him to Devil's Whip. I don't think he'll do anything to you."

"Right now," Tom said, "I want to get home and out of these wet clothes. That's all I can think about. I'll worry about the judge and the jury later."

"Good idea," Ben said. Tom got up to go and Ben stopped him. "Why didn't you go through with it, Tom? Why didn't you leave him up there? Not that I am all that against it."

Tom drained the last of the hot, strong coffee and said, "Guess I did it for Caroline. Guess I did it because you deputized me. Guess there was something I found up there in me that I thought I'd lost."

"See you in the morning," Ben said. Then he yawned and winked. "Make that the afternoon. I'm going to catch up on my shut-eye."

Tom took Jubal's rig back to the ranch. The snow had stopped and the wind had died down. Overhead the clouds had been swept away and there was a pale, three-quarter moon shining. It was bright enough for Tom to see his way home. All the way he kept thinking about Jubal and what he had done. He could have made something of his life, but he had choices like anyone else. He just made the wrong ones.

By the time Tom got home he was so sleepy

he could hardly unhitch the rig and rub the horses down. He finally made it to the house and when he opened the door there stood Madrid in the doorway of his bedroom.

All he said was, "Want to talk about it?"

"Tomorrow," Tom answered.

"See you then," Madrid said. Then, as he turned and went inside, "Is it all over?"

Tom nodded wearily. "It's all over."

Madrid didn't say anymore. Tom stripped down and crawled under the blankets on the floor and fell asleep.

Epilogue

The winter wind cried a mournful dirge around the carved headstone markers in the graveyard. It whispered in the weeds and tall withered grass that grew among the graves.

Tom Cardy stood before the grave that held the remains of his wife. Overhead the sky was boiling with snow-gorged clouds.

Slowly Tom removed his Stetson and bowed his head. Somewhere in the distance there was the cry of some feral animal but Tom scarcely heard it. He stood there for a few minutes before he said, "Rest well, Caroline."

Then Tom put his hat back on and, drawing the collar of his jacket closer to his neck, he walked away.